A Cowboy's Secret Crush

SWEET VIEW RANCH
BOOK THREE

JESSIE GUSSMAN

Contents

Acknowledgments   v

Chapter 1   1
Chapter 2   8
Chapter 3   15
Chapter 4   24
Chapter 5   30
Chapter 6   38
Chapter 7   47
Chapter 8   54
Chapter 9   59
Chapter 10   66
Chapter 11   73
Chapter 12   86
Chapter 13   93
Chapter 14   100
Chapter 15   106
Chapter 16   113
Chapter 17   120
Chapter 18   126
Chapter 19   134
Chapter 20   138
Chapter 21   144
Chapter 22   150
Chapter 23   159
Chapter 24   165
Chapter 25   172
Chapter 26   178
Chapter 27   183
Epilogue   190
Sneak Peek of A Cowboy's Heart of Gold   192

A Gift from Jessie   209
Escape to more faith-filled romance series by Jessie Gussman!   211

Acknowledgments

Cover art by Julia Gussman
Editing by Heather Hayden
Narration by Jay Dyess
Author Services by CE Author Assistant

***

Listen to the unabridged audio for FREE performed by Jay Dyess on the Say with Jay channel on YouTube. Get early access to all of Jay's recordings and listen to Jessie's books before they're available to the general public, plus get daily Bible readings by Jay and bonus scenes by becoming a Say with Jay channel member.

Chapter One

He had never kidnapped anyone before.

Asher Clybourn glanced across the seat at the woman sitting beside him. He wasn't sure she had stopped talking since they left Sweet Water, North Dakota, five hours ago.

Her phone had died shortly after they crossed the line from North Dakota into Montana. Ever since then, she'd been rotating between asking him how much longer until they got there, regaling him with stories of the latest movies and TV shows she watched, and despairing that she would ever get her phone plugged in and heartbroken because she was missing all the latest of her episodes.

Asher had not told her that where they were going, there would be no electricity.

He also had not told her that he had a charger in the console of his pickup.

She stopped talking for several seconds, and he glanced over to see if she was looking at him like she needed him to answer a question she just asked.

Her eyes pointed down at her hands which were clasped in her lap, so he figured he was off the hook. But his heart was troubled, just a little, because Sondra seemed so confident, so...worldly. But that little glance showed him that maybe some of it at least was a front. He'd never seen her look more insecure.

He swallowed, tightened his hold on the steering wheel, and spoke. "There's a rest stop up ahead. Do you need to stop?"

"Can we stay for an hour or so, so I can charge my phone?" Her eyes lifted hopefully, and her voice held suppressed excitement.

"No. We can't."

He wasn't being mean. Not on purpose. But if they wanted to get to his secluded mountain cabin before dark, they couldn't spend a lot of time sitting around. Although, he was going to have to stop in the last small town and grab some things at the grocery store. His cabin was stocked with some canned food, but Sondra seemed like the kind of woman who was used to having fresh produce and some of the finer things in life around her at all times.

He could provide those things for her. But she'd always been more interested in his older brother, Ezra, and had never given him a second glance.

Of course, when they were younger, that was totally understandable since she was four years older than he was, and in high school, a girl who was four years older didn't look back at a boy who was so much younger.

But now, now that they were adults, the age difference shouldn't matter. At least in his mind, it shouldn't.

But what did he know? He and his family had spent so much time trying to get their ranch profitable, and then with his parents dying in a car accident, they had even more on their plates, he hadn't really had time to learn what might or might not be important regarding age differences.

He could tell himself that was why Sondra was in the pickup with him. Because his loyalty was to his family, and his brother needed to focus on his new wife and not have his ex-fiancée in the picture. But Asher knew, deep down, that was a lie.

She was in the pickup with him now because of the crush he'd had on her for years. He had seen an opportunity for him to spend time with her, and he hadn't wanted to pass it up.

She hadn't said anything more since he'd denied her request to charge her phone, so he prompted her. "But if you need to stop to use the restroom, we can."

"How much longer until we get there?" she asked, and for the first time, he heard a little bit of...fear in her voice.

Immediately, he worked to combat whatever issues she was having.

"It'll only be another five or so hours. As long as we don't get caught up anywhere. I'll have to stop once for fuel, but I'll probably do that when we're closer." That way, he would have as full of a tank as he could when they headed to the mountains. There was no place to grab fuel for the last forty-five minutes of their trip.

He loved his cabin because it was remote. That had been the whole selling point of the property for him. He'd spent a lot of time building the cabin, and it was pretty nice now, if he did say so himself, even if it was very rustic.

What would Sondra think of it?

"Okay. Let's stop. I can probably get a drink even if I can't charge my phone. Did I mention that I'm missing all of my great shows?" she asked, and while her composure seemed to be back, he noted that her fingers played with the seam of her jeans, folding it and unfolding it as though she were nervous or upset.

Withdrawal would do that to a person.

Sondra was so hooked on her phone, her electronics, and her fictional characters that being without them was probably difficult. Asher didn't want to pretend to know what was best for her, but he figured probably any addiction that a person had had a tendency to draw them away from the Lord. After all, the only addiction that would be acceptable would be an addiction to God and His Word. Anything else was an idol.

That was kind of hard core, and he had a few idols in his own life he constantly tried to remove.

"All right. We'll stop. If you'd like me to get you something from the vending machine while you're in the restroom, I can. I think they probably have drinks and snack items."

"Do you think they'd have a fruit cup?" she asked, looking over at him hopefully.

He'd never had an affinity for blondes, or any particular hair color, because his affinity had always been for Sondra. Since she happened to be blonde, he would have said that was his favorite hair color. Her big green eyes blinked at him, and he had to be careful not to get caught by them, since he needed to keep his focus on the road. In North Dakota, with the miles upon miles of stick-straight roads, it wasn't quite as important, but since they'd hit the foothills, the road had gotten more curvy, and while not dangerous—or treacherous, the way he might term it as they got closer to the Rockies—it still took his full attention.

He didn't need to look at her to know what she looked like, though. The blonde hair, the emerald green eyes, the high cheekbones, and the full lips.

Of course, the rest of her looked pretty good too, although she wasn't skinny but more of a full-figured kind of girl. It was exactly how he liked her, and he wouldn't want her to change at all. He wasn't even sure that Ezra had ever noticed anything about her, and he wondered if he were to call his brother right now, if Ezra would even be able to say what color her hair was.

Asher had tried hard not to be jealous of his brother.

Ezra was commanding, the leader of their family, and Asher had the utmost respect for him and didn't have any issues with anything else in his brother's life, other than the fact that Ezra had Sondra, and he'd gotten her without even trying. She had been the one to chase after him, and he had simply stood there and allowed her to catch him.

It had made Asher angry the way Ezra didn't seem to care about her at all and the way she had seemed to fawn all over him.

But now that she was in his pickup, he didn't know what to say to her. He didn't want her to know that he knew so much about her, because that would be...a dead giveaway. A person didn't learn all there was to know about someone else just for the kicks and giggles.

Of course, he said to himself that he knew everything there was to know about her, but he knew that wasn't true. He knew everything she presented to the world, but he suspected there were deep pockets of things she kept hidden from the world. He wanted to know about those places too.

"If they have one, I can get it for you. What would be your second choice?"

"I don't want to eat a bunch of junk. I'm on a diet."

"What kind of diet?" he asked, knowing there was a difference in what she'd be able to eat. He had six sisters, so he wasn't completely oblivious to the ways of women.

"It's the twenty by three thousand by six and ten, no zucchini, no bread crusts, no papayas after six o'clock waterski diet."

"I see."

"Oh, you're familiar with it? Have you seen the TV show that features Apple Ciceron? She's the star who made the diet famous. Tell me you've heard of her!"

He didn't have a clue, although...had she said something about her earlier?

"You were talking about her earlier, weren't you?"

"You remember? Well! I didn't know you were listening to me. You looked so serious. Just like Jed Writ. He is tall, dark, and handsome, a bad-boy, silent, dark stubble on his chiseled jaw guy that all the girls fall in love with. That includes me." Her smile could light up his entire world, and it did now.

"Guess he's a lucky guy then," he said, although he didn't believe in luck. He believed in God, a God that created all things and controlled the universe with His words. In his opinion, if a person was a Christian, they didn't need luck, they just needed God.

"I guess you could say that. That would be from the man's perspective. Jiminy O'Reilly is always talking about the man's perspective on *Three Boots and a Delete*. Have you seen that show?"

"No. We don't have a TV."

"Oh, that's right. That's just crazy. Can you imagine growing up without a TV? Why, TV was my best friend when I was a kid."

He suspected as much. She knew all there was to know about it, because that's all she had to do. Her parents were absent at best. She already spent a lot of time out on their ranch in Wyoming where they grew up. She seemed to love his big family, and that was why he thought that she'd thrown herself at Ezra. He hoped it wasn't some kind of undying love that she felt for his brother, but more of the way she felt when she was around their family, and she wanted that for herself.

Asher wasn't usually that astute, but he spent a lot of time studying

Sondra. She'd been at their house a good bit, and while her attention had been mostly focused on Ezra, it had been good in a way for Asher since he had been able to study her without her knowing.

Of course, the more he figured out about her, the deeper his feelings ran.

Lord, I'm not doing the wrong thing, am I?

That was probably not a good prayer. His prayer should be more along the lines of, *Lord, show me Your will.* But he hadn't been able to pass up the opportunity of having Sondra all to himself.

"That's probably why you know so much about everything," he said casually, responding to her last statement. There had been a few moments of silence in his truck, which when a person was around Sondra, there wasn't much silence. He didn't mind. He enjoyed listening to her. He liked the tone of her voice. There was something about it that...made him smile. It just seemed to vibrate down through his chest, making him feel warm and happy inside.

"Really? You think I know a lot?"

"Yeah. I haven't heard of a show that you couldn't tell me all about."

"Well... Thanks. I do try to stay up on all the latest." Her smile was pleased and happy, like someone had finally noticed her. "In fact, did you hear about the latest Hollywood couple breaking up?"

"No. You gonna tell me about it?" he asked, even though he was less interested in hearing about a Hollywood breakup than he was in just listening to Sondra talk.

"Well, I certainly can, although I don't believe in cheating."

"No. That seems to be what a lot of the Hollywood people do. They hook up, then they break up. It's like a cycle." He lifted his shoulder. "I think once you get into that cycle, it's kind of hard to break it, because when things don't work out, your automatic answer is to break up."

"Oh. I hadn't ever thought of that." She was quiet for a few moments, like she was thinking about what he said. He felt a little hope bloom in his chest. He had never tried to talk to her about anything, and the idea that she was weighing his words and believing them made him feel a little bolder.

"Isn't that true?" he asked, without really expecting an answer. "When breaking up is the solution to your problems, divorce is the first thing you look at when your marriage doesn't go the way you think it should."

"Well, it's true that there are a lot of Hollywood couples that don't stay together. In fact, I can only name a few who have." And then she started ticking them off on her fingers.

He listened, although he didn't recognize any of the names. He supposed if he spent enough time with her, he would start knowing these people the same way she did. She talked about them like they were her friends. Like she knew them personally. And that was just kind of odd, since to his knowledge, she had never met any of them. It was so weird to think of a complete stranger as someone who was...close to you.

Again, he thought about her upbringing and the fact that she hadn't seemed to have too many people who cared about her, so it maybe was understandable that she got so invested in the lives of people she didn't even know.

Maybe, maybe if he could play his cards right, she could get invested in him.

Chapter Two

"All right. I'll walk you in, sometimes these places can be dangerous."

Sondra's heart started to thump in her chest. "Dangerous?"

"I didn't mean to scare you. Just... There are a lot of people who pass through rest areas, and not all of them are good people."

"All right. I believe you." Her very own TV adventure! She couldn't believe it. She'd basically been swept away, kidnapped by a person she barely knew. Well. That was a bit of an exaggeration. She'd known Asher since he was a kid. He was a lot younger than she was, and she never really paid a whole lot of attention to him, but still, that kind of made him a stranger. And he kidnapped her! It was so...*Hollywood.*

Now, they were going to a dangerous place where he would have to protect her.

She almost rubbed her hands together in glee. This was better than TV! It was the first time in her life she'd actually thought her real life was better than the life that she watched on the screen.

Of course, she still missed her phone and felt a sense of unease as the online world went on without her.

She couldn't follow all of her TokBok personalities, and she couldn't check in and give an update on BookFace. Her Instant was going to be sadly out of date by the time she got her phone charged, and all of her other socials were going to need to be completely overhauled when she got back online.

Although, she would have a great story to tell. Typically, her life was extremely boring, and the most exciting thing that had ever happened to her, getting engaged to Ezra, had blown up in her face today.

Thankfully, she had been more in love with the idea of being in love with Ezra than she had been in love with the man himself.

She hadn't realized that until he'd broken up with her and she'd been enjoying the drama. In fact, she enjoyed the drama so much that his calm, rational words over the phone weren't nearly enough for her.

She had to drive from Wyoming to North Dakota to confront him. Just like a Hollywood movie star.

It had been the most exciting thing she'd done in ages.

Asher pulled his truck to a stop, and she got out carefully, looking around to see where the dangerous people might be. Two spaces down from them, a family gathered around their SUV, grabbing snacks out of a bag and running off to a picnic table.

It was a little cold to have a picnic, in her opinion anyway, but the kids looked happy and relieved to be out of the car for a while.

She really didn't know what that was like. Grabbing snacks out of the bag, having a mom who cared enough to pack some, or having siblings. Maybe it didn't matter if it was cold outside if you had brothers and sisters around you talking and laughing.

They didn't look dangerous though.

There were two people walking dogs over in the side area that was designated for that, and several older couples, past retirement age if she were any judge, strolling either to or from the restrooms. She tried to fight back disappointment. There was no one to be afraid of. Nothing that looked dangerous seemed to be lurking around. There wasn't even a dog off its leash.

Then, in her rearview mirror she saw a man getting out of his big truck, which was parked in the designated area, slamming the door shut before striding toward the restroom. It was a large man, dark, with a chain hanging down from his belt loop, slapping on his leg as he walked, and she assumed it was attached to his wallet in his back pocket.

Now that was definitely a scary-looking guy.

"Asher. Wait for me," she said as she slammed her door shut and hurried around the side of the truck to where Asher stood in front of it.

"You're right. This does seem like a dangerous place," she said as she slipped her arm in his and walked closely beside him as he started toward the restrooms.

"You have to be careful at night, but usually this time in late afternoon, they're not too bad."

"Oh, I feel so much safer with you beside me. I mean, you look like the kind of person who could win a fistfight." She blinked her eyes up at him. She'd never seen any of the Clybourn family in any kind of fight, but it sounded good anyway.

It made him smile too. Or it was more of a curvy grin that made a dimple she'd never noticed pop in his cheek.

"I didn't know you had a dimple!" she said before she thought about it. That it wasn't really something that a heroine would say to the leading man in a movie.

"Yeah. All my life. It's been right there."

She giggled. Asher was so funny. He was young and not her type at all, since he didn't have the gorgeous looks of a Hollywood movie star, he didn't even have the commanding carriage of his brother, Ezra. Ezra had the looks and the carriage, and he was an older man. That all made him very appealing.

But Asher was what she had, so she had to work with it. Even if this talent wasn't quite what she was used to.

"Well, it's adorable," she said, turning from looking at him to scanning the area again. Two older ladies walked out together, chatting about visiting their grandchild and crocheting something, which did not give her any good material to work with.

"I'm gonna run into the restroom while you're in, but I'm sure I'll be out before you. I'll wait right here."

"Oh, thank you. I'll hurry. It's scary here." That was definitely a bit of an exaggeration, because other than the truck driver coming in behind them, she hadn't seen anything that was the slightest bit scary, and no offense to that fella, but she was pretty sure even in her out-of-shape condition, she could outrun that dude.

That thought wasn't romantic or fun at all, so she pushed it aside and pretended that he was more in shape than what he actually was.

Asher patted her hand, and she gave him a tremulous smile before she went to the ladies' restroom.

There wasn't anything scary in there, just a few older ladies and a mom with a couple little kids. Sondra smiled at them as she walked to her stall, wondering what in the world Asher had planned.

She did appreciate him sweeping her out of the situation and appreciated the drama that it brought to her life, but...she missed her phone. A little curl of fear pooled in her midsection. Her phone, and her focus on all the shows and social media, kept the fear at bay.

She should have brought it in so she could plug it in and charge it for even five minutes while she used the restroom. That would be enough to get her online for a bit, and she could catch up on the latest and not get so far behind. It was going to take her forever to get caught back up on all of her shows and social media.

Plus, her followers were going to miss her.

Not that she had that many. How could she? She never did anything interesting. Her monologues with her opinion about what was happening on all of the latest sitcoms and reality shows weren't any different than anyone else's online. And hadn't really gained any traction.

It didn't take any time at all, and she was washing her hands and leaving the restroom.

True to his word, Asher was waiting for her, and to her surprise, he held a fruit cup.

"I didn't even see the vending machines," she said, looking around.

"They were over there. This was the only thing that looked healthy. I also grabbed you a bottle of water." He pulled it out from underneath his arm.

"Oh. Thank you." She hadn't asked for that, but now that she thought about it, she was kind of thirsty. She hadn't been anticipating his thoughtfulness. If she couldn't find danger in the restroom, it would be nice if she could make her captor a villain, that would keep her mind occupied so it didn't have room for the fearful thoughts of reality, but Asher wasn't playing his part very well.

"Would you like anything else?" he asked, very solicitous and kind.

"No. This is perfect. If I can't have my phone, at least I have fruit and water," she said, laughing a little, even though she didn't think it was very funny.

He did that whole curvy lip thing, where his dimple came out, and she found herself looking at it again. Cute. She hadn't known that Asher had a dimple.

They walked back to the truck, with her tucking her hand in his arm again, walking close. Even though she hadn't really seen anything that was remotely dangerous, it was fun and distracting to pretend that the possibility was there. And Asher seemed to be willing to allow her her little fantasy.

She wouldn't say he encouraged it, but he did pay a little bit more attention to her than Ezra ever had. Ezra not paying attention to her didn't really bother her. She mostly figured he was listening and just didn't show it. But considering how easily he threw her aside, maybe he wasn't and she had built castles in the air around him. That wouldn't be the first time she built castles in the air.

To her surprise, Asher went to her side of the pickup and opened her door for her.

"My goodness. Thank you. What a surprise. How gallant." She couldn't help it. He had charmed her with that gesture. She couldn't remember anyone ever opening her door before. She and Ezra hardly ever went anywhere, and when they did, Ezra was usually working from his phone. The man never stopped. Of course she understood, since he was the head of his household and had extra responsibilities since his parents had died in a car accident, but this attention was nice.

"My pleasure," he said easily, waiting until she had herself tucked in before he closed the door.

She could almost feel like the heroine in the movie, and not the victim, with that type of treatment.

He didn't mess around but was back on the road immediately, merging into traffic and getting up to highway speed.

She noticed then that he hadn't gotten anything for himself.

"Aren't you hungry?"

"Nah." Then he huffed out a little laugh and glanced over across the seat. "That's not true. I'm always hungry, but I can wait."

"I could wait too," she said, not realizing that waiting was a thing.

"No. It wasn't a slam or anything. I was glad to get you something. I just...didn't want anything. I guess. I'm looking forward to getting to the cabin, and I'll think about eating then. Although we'll pick up groceries first before we get there."

"Oh. We can't just run to the grocery store after we get there?"

"No. The closest grocery store is an hour away. On a good day. And it's not open all the time. I actually like to stop at a bigger grocery store which is even farther from the cabin, but I try to give the little one business just to keep it in business, I guess."

She nodded, although she didn't really understand. She supposed there were benefits to having grocery stores as close as possible to his cabin. But she couldn't imagine wanting to be somewhere where she was an hour away from a store. That was crazy.

"So... You don't seem overly heartbroken about Ezra," Asher said, and his eyes stayed fixed on the road, like he was just making casual conversation. Or maybe he was concerned about her and was a little embarrassed about it. That sounded better, so she thought she'd go with that. She appreciated being able to talk. Normally her phone and her shows were able to keep her anxiety in check, but in lieu of them, she needed something else to focus on. She could feel herself getting antsy.

"I think I was more in love with the idea of being in love with him than I was actually in love with him, if that makes sense," she said as casually as she could as she peeled the top of her fruit cup back.

"Oh, I grabbed this," Asher said, leaning forward and reaching into his back pocket, pulling out a plastic fork that was still in a clear package.

"Oh. I guess it hadn't even occurred to me yet how I was going to eat. Thank you." She felt a little helpless. He was doing everything to provide for her, and she hadn't done a thing to think for herself.

But that was the way the heroine was supposed to be. Let the hero think for her, while she just worried about looking good.

Unless of course she was the heroine of an action movie, and then she had to wear skintight muscle shirts, and guns strapped across both shoulders, and a knife in her combat boots.

That wasn't the type of heroine she was. She was more of the *Angel Jeffries's Diary* heroine, a little frumpy but lovable.

"I was just wondering. I didn't want you sitting over there dying inside because I'm pushing you to go away when you don't feel capable of moving because of your heartbreak."

"No. I... I really am disappointed. I guess that's the right word though, disappointed. I'm not really crushed or heartbroken. Which, I suppose, shows more than anything else that it probably wasn't meant to be, and...I just built air castles about us, and it's going to take a little bit of time to get over that."

He nodded, and she wasn't sure whether he understood or not.

"It's kind of like that show, *Cowboy in the City*. Have you seen that one?"

"No."

Of course he hadn't. He already told her that he didn't watch TV. Didn't even have one. Which she knew, and...it had never bothered her when she was there that there was no TV set at their house. She spent a lot of time with them when she was a teen and her early twenties. There was always so much going on that their family really didn't need a TV. That was just extra noise.

Regardless, the ever-present anxiety shivered under her ribs, so she launched into a monologue about *Cowboy in the City* and how that applied to her situation.

Asher didn't seem to care; in fact, if she had to guess, it was almost like he liked listening to her. That was all the encouragement she needed to continue on for the next hundred miles or so.

Chapter Three

Asher pulled off the interstate, and the woman beside him stirred. He smiled, because he found it a little funny that she had talked herself to sleep.

Seriously, she had still been talking when her eyes started closing and her words had started slurring together.

He wasn't precious about his truck, thankfully, because the fruit cup that she'd been holding had tilted a little, and some of the syrup ran out. He'd taken it gently from her hand, and she hadn't even noticed.

He had noticed. Noticed that her fingers were curvy like the rest of her. Not slender and long, but he wouldn't call them short either. They just...had character, personality.

He liked that and thought it described her hands rather well. They were white, with no calluses. He doubted she'd ever done a day's manual labor in her life, not that he knew of anyway. Even when she was at their house, she did more talking than anything. But someone who was able to talk was usually good company. As long as she didn't expect him to answer her every other sentence, which Sondra didn't.

She'd been content to pretty much talk to herself for the first hundred miles after the rest area, until she'd fallen asleep.

He tried to ease the truck gently to the stop sign, without waking her up. Although, it might be better if she did wake up. She'd sleep better that night if she hadn't slept all day. Although, he supposed breaking up with someone was stressful, even if it hadn't been as painful as what he feared.

It had done his heart good to hear her say that she hadn't been in love with Ezra. Just in love with the idea of being in love. Which, he'd never heard about or even considered that a person could do such a thing, but he believed Sondra when she said that described her.

"Where are we?" Sondra murmured as she straightened, the fork falling out of her fingers and onto the floor, although she didn't notice. They'd driven into the mountains since her eyes had closed, and it must feel like she was in a completely different place.

"We're close. About two hours away. We're stopping at that grocery store in the next hour, if you can wait that long to stop again?"

Normally, on the ranch and with his siblings, he didn't have a problem saying what needed to be said, but somehow asking Sondra if she needed to use the restroom was a little...much.

Either she didn't understand his question, or she didn't have to go, because she said, "I'm fine."

"You had quite a nap."

"Yeah. I...forgot where I was there for a little bit."

"There's so much going on in your head, I would think that you'd get a little confused about reality versus your imagination anyway."

Her head snapped around to him, and her eyes widened. The dash lights cast an odd-looking glow on her face. Her eyes were dark gray, rather than the emerald green he knew them to be. But he couldn't mistake the look of shock on her face.

"I can't believe you said that."

He said something wrong? He glanced at her, then back at the road. He knew the way by heart and wasn't worried about missing any roads, whether it was dark or not. But the roads around here definitely needed a person to pay close attention, and he couldn't stare at her the way he wanted to.

"Did I offend you?" He took a breath. "I'm sorry. I didn't mean to."

"No. You just... You hit the nail right on the head. I'm...shocked that you would have seen."

He lifted his shoulder, trying to make it seem like it wasn't a big deal, but her words had struck fear into his heart. He didn't want her to know how much he knew about her. After all, it was almost stalker-ish the way he had studied her over the years and figured her out. At least tried to.

"I'm sorry. That just seems obvious to me. You're always talking about stories and the things you watch on TV. I just assumed your head must be bursting with those kinds of thoughts."

"Yeah. It is. I have trouble keeping it contained sometimes. I suppose you noticed that I have a tendency to talk a lot."

He tried not to laugh at that. It was like the understatement of the year. Anyone who could talk themselves to sleep definitely talked a lot.

"Yeah. But I don't mind listening to you. Your voice sounds...nice." That was all he should say. He shouldn't tell her that it felt warm and smooth in his soul somehow, and made him feel less...alone. Not that a person with eleven siblings could ever feel alone.

Maybe that was why he'd gotten his cabin in the mountains. So that he could enjoy some solitude once in a while. But the idea of bringing Sondra to it probably should make him feel like someone would be invading his privacy, but he found himself eager to have her there. He wasn't sure why.

"Thanks. I don't think I've ever had a compliment on my voice before. Although I have had a few people say that it was grating and annoying..." she trailed off. Like the thought of those people made her sad.

"I guess they just didn't know what a good voice sounds like." He wanted to make her feel better. But he didn't want to give her lies that weren't true. He wasn't lying about her voice though. He loved listening to her. "I guess different folks like different things. But for me, you can talk all you want to, and I'll enjoy it."

"Well. I don't think anyone's ever said that to me before." She looked down at her lap, like she knew she talked a lot, and it was something that had bothered her. Or maybe it bothered her that it bothered other people, he wasn't sure.

He'd never really had a problem with talking a lot. In fact, if anything, sometimes he didn't say enough. He was working on it. He found that he could avoid a lot of misunderstandings if he'd just open his mouth and speak. Or sometimes just open his mouth and ask questions. Because sometimes the things that he made assumptions about were totally wrong.

"I figured we'd stay in the mountains for a week. Does that sound okay to you?" He held his breath. Maybe he should have tried to lead up to that a little better, but he'd been spending the last hour while she slept trying to figure out how to tell her that he wanted to stay at least a week. He'd rather stay two or three. He was pretty sure, while the ranch could use his help, that Ezra would appreciate the time with his new wife. Hopefully by the time he brought Sondra back, Ezra and Alaska would be situated, and even more hopefully, Sondra wouldn't be interested in Ezra anymore anyway.

Asher figured he needed at least a week. But he'd like to have more.

"A week?" Sondra said.

"I'd like to. I need to get groceries. We don't have to make a firm decision, but once I go up, I typically don't go back down until I need to make another grocery run. It's a long drive, and I don't come out here to drive around. I come out here to...get away." He almost didn't say that last part. That was a little more of himself than he wanted to reveal. Sure, he had a crush on Sondra, but he didn't know how she felt about him, and he couldn't just share his hopes and dreams and the secret things he thought about with just anyone.

"That's funny. I view it as a special privilege to get to spend time with your family, and you find an entire cabin just so you can get away. It's interesting that people have different goals and different things they consider to be good."

"Don't get me wrong. I love my family. I really do. And I love spending time with them. And I love being on the ranch and working there."

"I see. I guess I feel like if that were my family, I'd never want to leave. I've heard other people say it's kind of crazy the way you guys are always together, but I totally get that. It's...unusual, but really cool."

He nodded. He didn't think that anyone in his family had actually planned that. They just always all pitched together on the farm. Trying to make it a success. Every one of the kids knew that their parents needed them to make ends meet. And then, when they lost their parents as they had been contemplating moving to a larger location to accommodate them all, everything had seemed to solidify, and he hadn't really considered doing anything other than working in the family business.

But Sondra had not said whether or not a week was okay. He was just going to assume that it was rather than ask again and risk her saying that she didn't want to go at all or that she wanted to turn around. He could see her fidgeting again, and he assumed it was because when she woke up normally, the first thing she did was to check her socials and get updates on all of the important things in her life, which were really stars and TV shows.

Maybe he was a little bit jealous of the time she spent doing that, but he realized that was a part of her, and...he kind of liked it in a weird way. Considering that he had no clue what she was talking about most of the time.

"If you have any particular groceries that you want, start thinking about it. We'll be stopping here shortly, and I'd like to do it without taking up too much time. I'm going to have a little bit of work to do once we hit the cabin."

He hadn't been planning on coming to the cabin again for a while. Spring was the busiest time of year on the ranch, except for possibly fall calving and harvesting. And he normally wouldn't consider leaving. He had stayed at the cabin for a few weeks over the winter a couple of different times. And when he left, he usually left a small stockpile of firewood, but typically he cut most of his firewood the first time he went to the cabin in the winter and then burned it throughout the year. He didn't normally let much sit there over the summer.

"I was just going to ask you to give me your phone number and I would text you a list, but...I guess I can't since my phone is dead."

"It's okay, we can do it the old-fashioned way. There is a pencil and a notebook in the glove box, if you want to get it out and write down whatever you want."

"What are we eating?" she asked, and he wasn't sure exactly what she was saying, except...

"Are you asking who's going to cook?" There was humor in his tone. He was teasing her a little bit, but he didn't think he was wrong.

"I guess it was kind of a roundabout way of doing that. I... I don't want to ask you to get a bunch of groceries when you already have meals planned."

"I don't have too many meals planned. There are only a few things I make, and I just have a tendency to repeat them."

"They must be pretty special meals."

"Well, one of my favorites is Sad Eyes Chicken. It's almost a tradition for me that it's my first meal when I go up every time."

"You have traditions at your cabin. Interesting. That's...not something I would have expected."

"From me or from life in general?" Was she thinking that she knew him a little bit? The thought made his mood lift, and he wanted to smile. But he thought maybe he was reading too much into it.

"You. I guess. Maybe that was a little presumptuous of me to think that I know you at all, but—"

"No. I didn't think that at all. I was just surprised. I didn't know if you thought I was a type or something."

"Well, there really isn't any Hollywood hero that's just like you. I mean, you're so much younger than me, sorry, but I never really paid attention to you before, but as I was thinking about it now, you just don't really fit into the Hollywood mold."

Well, that was hurtful. She just flat-out admitted that she never really paid attention to him. But, he reminded himself, that was why he had her. So that they could go up together and spend some time together, and maybe she would notice him for more than the younger kid that ran around and probably annoyed her.

"I guess I like being unique. I'll take that."

"Good. It was mostly a compliment. I mean, when there is no mold, you can make your own. Like George Henry and Kayden Bigelow."

Those names didn't mean anything to him; he didn't recognize them at all. But he nodded. "So other people don't quite fit the stereotypical Hollywood mold, and they're successful anyway?"

"Yeah. You could be too. I mean, if your dream is to be a Hollywood movie star."

"No. I've only ever wanted to be on my family's ranch with my siblings, although I guess my parents were always in the picture too."

"They were really great parents. I was always so jealous."

"Really?" That shouldn't surprise him. He knew what her parents were like. Not interested or involved in her life much at all.

"Yeah. You always seemed to have the perfect family."

"Perfect, except for the fact that there were twelve of us. That kind of blows perfect out of the water."

"I guess it was pretty unusual, but it always seemed like you guys had so much fun. And your parents were awesome."

"Yeah. I still miss them."

"Has it really been ten years?" she asked softly, carefully, almost as though she was afraid that she was going to offend him.

He lifted a shoulder. "It's okay. They're dead, and there's nothing I can do about it. Yeah, it's been a little over ten years."

"My parents are still alive, but I haven't talked to them in... Since last Christmas, I guess. Typically we get together over the holidays; that's when they usually remember they have a kid. Although this past Christmas, they went snorkeling in the Caribbean and took a month-long vacation from Thanksgiving through the New Year. I... I had a movie marathon on Thanksgiving and ate soup from a can. And on Christmas, I wrapped myself up a couple of presents and opened them while watching all of my favorite Christmas movies for twenty-four hours straight."

That was sad. He hadn't realized she was alone over the holidays.

"Why didn't Ezra invite you to our family Christmas?" It made him mad at his brother. How could Ezra allow her to be alone like that?

"I don't think Ezra knew. I mean, I asked him about getting together, and he just always talked about how much work he had to do. It...makes him sound like a jerk now, but...I think maybe we were only together because I insisted on it. I can't really get mad at him for not caring about me when I didn't care about him and insisted that we were engaged when we...really weren't, I guess."

Asher's hands gripped the steering wheel. He wanted to strangle his brother, but he also wanted to comfort Sondra somehow. But he didn't know how. And he really didn't have that right. It was like she just said, it wouldn't mean anything if she didn't want him to. The way she didn't mean anything to Ezra, since he didn't want her.

Still, rejection hurt, no matter what direction it came from.

He thought maybe a subject change was in order. "I told you I always cook my Sad Eyes Chicken. It's basically baked chicken breast with some spinach and cheese mixture over the top. Sometimes I dip it in mayonnaise."

"That sounds really good."

"It's the one thing I have a recipe written down for the cabin. Everything else, I kind of just wing it, but I really like that."

"It would be really cool to have a cooking channel on YouTube or something. I think it would be fun. I just...don't really have anyone to cook for, and it's no fun to just cook for myself. Everyone you see has a cooking channel for families or for company or for whatever, and I'm kind of sad, since it's just me."

"I think you'd be surprised how many single people there are who cook for just one and maybe even seek out channels where the creators are making meals for just one person."

He had no idea, but he did know that there were a lot of people who lived by themselves, and it wasn't that big of a deal. It wasn't sad and didn't have to be lonely either.

But Sondra seemed more like an extrovert, and maybe the way she'd grown up, with TV filling in the gaps of her loneliness, had kept her from making real-life friends.

Or maybe it was the idea that their family was there for her whenever she needed them, and then they'd moved to North Dakota, and she really was alone.

Of course, her business designing websites, one she did from home, wasn't exactly conducive to getting out and making friends.

"How long did you take off from your job?" he asked, realizing that that might be a factor.

"I just finished designing a website, which I originally thought was perfect timing, since I wanted to go and confront Ezra. I didn't have anything else lined up. And I didn't try to get anything, because of being on the road."

"All right. Then we'll just play it by ear. We'll get enough groceries so we don't starve. Sound good?" he asked as he made the last turn to head into town.

They talked a bit more about the groceries that they needed to get, and he found that Sondra was pleasant and a little funny. It surprised him, since he thought of her as a person who always talked about the latest TV shows and movies. The idea that she could hold a regular conversation wasn't exactly surprising, but...he just didn't usually get to see it. Maybe his sisters had, since they spent more time with her than he had, or Ezra, although he doubted it. Since Ezra had seemed oblivious to Sondra.

Of course, maybe that was a good thing, since Ezra was definitely not oblivious to Alaska, the woman he had just married. That's the way life was supposed to be. A man paid attention to the woman he got married to. Other women really shouldn't be on his radar.

For him, that had been totally true. Sondra had been the only woman he thought about for...years, if ever. Now, God had given him this one, short chance to get her to notice him. He hoped he didn't mess it up.

Chapter Four

For Sondra, grocery shopping had always been a necessary evil. She hadn't realized how much fun it could be when she went shopping with another person. Although, maybe it was just Asher.

"What are these?" he asked, holding up a jar of pickled garlic, instead of the black olives he was supposed to grab.

"That's garlic. Can't you see the garlic?"

"That's weird. People eat this?" he asked, tilting the jar and looking at it like he'd never seen garlic before.

"They do. It's actually pretty good. Although, married people really should stay away from it, because when you eat garlic, everybody around you knows it."

"So, isn't this supposed to keep vampires away?"

"Oh my goodness, you've seen the show *Vampires and the Cowboy*?"

"No. I just heard about it. Because you know I live on earth."

She laughed. "Give me that." She grabbed the jar from his hand and put it back on the shelf.

"Wait. Shouldn't we, you know, have a little bit of garlic at the cabin. Just in case, you know. Vampires."

"Oh my goodness. You are ridiculous." She watched as he took it back off the shelf and put it in the cart.

"Maybe you should focus on getting something practical, like mousetraps. Are there mice at the cabin?" She only thought to ask this because *Cowboy in the Cabin*, the show she binged shamelessly between Christmas and New Year's, had had one episode where they had been overrun with mice.

"I don't know. I've never noticed. I suppose it might be. What can we get to eat that will keep mice away the same way garlic keeps vampires away?"

"How about we just do mousetraps?"

"Too bad there aren't vampire traps," he said as they slowly strolled down the aisle. The grocery store was pretty much empty, and Sondra had noticed the sign on the door that said it closed before nine, which she thought was crazy. Of course, growing up in Wyoming, she knew all about stores that closed by 9 o'clock. Most people were in bed at that point, although the culture around her was changing.

Not that she noticed overmuch. Since she usually paid more attention to the show she was binging than the actual people around her.

"The one rule is you have to have junk food."

"No. We're changing the rules. You can't drive me away to your cabin in the mountains and then feed me junk food. Do you see this, this does not need junk food," she said, pointing to her waist which had about thirty pounds more on it than what she really wanted it to. But it didn't seem to matter how much she dieted, it never came off.

"I think that looks perfect. Let's get the junk food," he said flippantly, grabbing a bag of potato chips. "Is this your favorite kind?"

"That kind's gross," she said, laughing and snatching the bag back out of his hand, careful not to crumple the chips. She set it back.

"If you're going to get chips, this is the kind you get." She pulled up the pickles and vinegar chips.

"That doesn't even sound good," he said as he looked at it, wrinkling up his nose. "And the bag is green. Who would look at a green bag of potato chips and think that anything inside it could possibly taste the slightest bit good?"

"I guess that's true. Green isn't exactly an appetizing color for potato chips."

"No. It's gross."

"Still, you've got to taste these. I bet you haven't even tried them."

"Busted." He looked a little abashed, and his dimple came out. She'd forgotten about it, and her eye got caught on it. For a moment, she forgot they were bantering back and forth and she was having a good time. That dimple. It was...adorable.

"Do I have something on my face?" he asked, after a moment where she hadn't said anything. And he just stood there, waiting.

She shook her head, mentally giving herself a shake as well. This was Asher. Ezra's little brother. Why was she staring at him like he was... someone special?

"A nose? It's rather large. Kinda cute. Although your dimple, that really steals the show right there."

"The dimple steals the show of my face? Is that what you just said?" Asher said as they moseyed up the aisle and turned the corner, coming to the dairy section.

"Yeah. We've got to skip this aisle. Everything here is fattening."

"That is good," he said, pointing to the cream cheese. "You can't go wrong right there. You can put that in everything. There, when you start your cooking channel, I just gave you my secret tip that will make everything you make wildly popular."

"Cream cheese? That's your secret tip?"

"Yep." He grabbed the box, pretended to think about it, then grabbed another. She laughed. Definitely, grocery shopping was much more fun with Asher.

"So, when we go home, you're going to have to come to my house every week and take me grocery shopping, so instead of it being something that I dread, you make it enjoyable. I don't think I've ever laughed this much in...ever."

"Well, I'm glad I'm entertaining. But I was actually being serious about the cream cheese. You can't go wrong with it."

"So, you pretended that you were going to make healthy meals, but everything's going to have cream cheese, and so it's not going to be healthy."

"Listen, you can use healthy ingredients, and that's fine, but even food has to have fun."

"Food has to have fun?" She snorted. "That's rich."

"It's true. No one wants to eat boring meals all the time. I mean, you know, if you're going to die, you might as well die happy or at least with a happy stomach."

"Or happy taste buds. This doesn't make everyone's stomach happy." She eyed the cream cheese as he set another box in the cart, making a total of three. "Let's compromise and get one."

"That is not a compromise. A compromise would be four." He reached for another container.

"No!" The word came out a little louder than she was expecting it to. She looked around, seeing that one shopper had turned their attention from the items of food in front of them to glance curiously at the woman who couldn't seem to keep her voice down in the grocery store. She lowered it to a stage whisper. "You're absolutely not going to eat four blocks of cream cheese in the next week. If we even stay a week."

His humor and his banter had taken her mind off the idea that she would be without her phone for an entire week. It wasn't that she was so addicted to her phone, it was that her friends online, both real and the ones that she knew and admired, movie stars and actresses and social media influencers, kept her company, kept her from being lonely, and kept the fear at bay.

A trickle of anxiety went through her, enough to make the smile slip from her face. She'd been in the grip of severe anxiety before, and the only thing that helped her was the relief she found in her shows and movies. Maybe it was fake friendships, fake relief, but it helped.

"What's the matter? If it's really going to upset you, I'll put them all back." There was still a little bit of humor in Asher's tone, but his eyes showed his concern as he looked down at her, studying her, trying to figure out what the issue was.

That kind of scrutiny, that kind of care, warmed her heart, and she forgot about her anxiety as she put her hand over top of the package in his, gripped it, and threw it in their cart.

His brows rose as he looked from her face to the package and back to her face. "Wow. Way to walk on the wild side." That curled-up grin, the one that did funny things to her stomach, appeared, and his dimple grinned at her as he said, "How about six? Can we do six?"

"This is not an auction."

He just laughed, grabbed two more packages, and threw them in.

"I'm going to assume we're having company," she said, lifting her nose into the air and blinking her eyes just a bit, pretending that she was not giving up.

"No company," he said, his grin only getting bigger.

She just lifted her brows and waited until he started to walk away, then she grabbed two more packages and tossed them in on top of his.

He laughed so loud the lady who had looked at her gave him a disapproving stare as well.

"Oh my goodness, you're going to get us thrown out. Be quiet."

"This is a grocery store, not church. I'm allowed to laugh."

"You're disturbing people who came here to shop in peace."

"I'm no louder than someone who came here with their kids. We're good. Aren't we?" he said, nodding to the lady who apparently couldn't resist that dimple, either, because her stern look turned into a smile.

"You two are so adorable. Young love is the best." She gave them a benevolent smile and then turned back toward the shelves.

Young love? There was no love. This was an abduction.

"I should tell her you kidnapped me," Sondra said, and Asher snorted.

"Yeah. She might change her mind about what's going on. It's not young love."

"Obviously not," she said, but she was a little disappointed. Part of her wanted to think that he had taken her because...he liked her. But she knew how closely the Clybourn family stuck together. It had nothing to do with him liking her and everything to do with him wanting to do something kind for his brother Ezra. Thinking that he would get the ex-fiancée out of the way so that Ezra could focus on his new wife. Yeah, it was a family thing.

That sucked her good humor right out of her, and she said to Asher, "Tell me what I can go get, and we'll split up. It'll be faster that way."

There was surprise on his face as he turned toward her, then confusion.

But her tone brokered no argument, and he agreed, saying the word slowly, "Okay."

She waited, and he gave her a list of two or three things that were from the freezer section. She walked away, feeling the loss. She'd been having such a good time with him, she wished reality hadn't imposed. But that was the story of her life. She got lost in her fictional worlds, and they were so much a part of her they felt real. Then, she got yanked back to reality, where things were never as nice as they were in her make-believe world.

They finished their shopping, checked out, and as she helped Asher put the groceries in the back of the truck, she thought maybe she should tell him that she wanted to go home. She felt a little bad doing that, because he'd bought enough groceries to last them for a week, but...it was going to be hard to sink back into the idea that he wasn't doing this for anything other than Ezra.

In other words, he didn't really care about her. He was just pretending.

That, along with the fact she couldn't charge her phone, almost made her open her mouth, and she couldn't really say why she didn't. The idea of going out to a remote cabin, of being away from her shows, caused her to tense up in anxiety, but...maybe it was something she needed.

That thought nagged at her, and she kept her mouth closed, getting in her side of the pickup while Asher returned the cart, and, for once, sitting quietly on her side while they drove deeper and deeper into the woods.

Chapter Five

Asher put the last of the groceries away. He didn't have too many modern conveniences, but a gas-operated refrigerator and freezer was one of them. He cooked on a woodstove, and there was no washer and dryer. But there was a creek nearby, and the few times he'd stayed long enough to need clean clothes, it had worked just fine to wash his clothes there.

It was cold, freezing actually, most of the year, but water was water, and it worked for him.

However, he wasn't really thinking about that as he closed the refrigerator door and turned back toward the table where Sondra sat, holding her dead phone in her hands and being just as quiet as she had been since they left the grocery store.

Something happened in the grocery store, although Asher wasn't sure what. But she had gone from funny and fun to...sullen and quiet.

He thought they'd been having a good time. He thought she'd been enjoying him, and he'd certainly been enjoying her. She was actually talking about things that didn't have anything to do with the shows she loved, and as he had known, she had a great personality that made him laugh and which he enjoyed.

He'd never been grocery shopping where he had such a good time. He figured he'd never go again without thinking of her.

He also had no idea what he was going to do with eight packages of cream cheese, but he felt like it was worth the extra money he'd spent, just to see her smile.

Maybe he'd set one on the table and pretend it was breakfast in the morning. Cut a block in half and put one half on her plate and a half on his, pour them each a glass of milk. Breakfast is served.

The thought should have made him smile, but it didn't, not really, because she still sat there, flipping her phone around. Maybe she wasn't going to be able to handle this after all. He'd had his doubts to begin with, since he knew she never disconnected.

He had enough wood for a fire for tonight, although he hadn't started to build one. It was chilly, and he needed to. He also should probably go out and chop some more firewood so they had some for the next day. Here in the mountains, it had a tendency to take a while to warm up, cool down fast, and sometimes not get as warm as a person thought it should.

In other words, he was afraid Sondra would get cold, and he didn't want that to happen.

He didn't want her to be miserable. That would defeat his purpose. He didn't want to offer to take her back, but he didn't see any other solution. If that's what she wanted, that's what he would do.

"Are you okay?" he asked, hoping maybe he was wrong, and it wasn't because she wanted to go home that she had been so quiet.

"I'm fine."

He almost laughed. From having sisters, he knew that "I'm fine" didn't really mean a person was fine. It meant *there is something seriously wrong, but I'm not going to tell you unless you ask the right questions.* Or maybe it was *I'm not going to tell you until I know that you're really interested, because I don't want to bare my heart to someone who doesn't really care.*

He had a lot of things to do, he wanted to get things ready for her, and it was already late, but again, maybe his sisters had taught him that sometimes a person just needed to take time.

Or maybe that was his mom. She always seemed to have time for him, no matter how busy she was with his siblings, even when she had a baby or toddlers running around, which had to have been hard. She made time for him.

He walked over, pulled out a chair at the end of the table, right beside where she was sitting, and sat down.

"I have sisters. I know that 'I'm fine' doesn't mean you're actually fine."

"Ezra has sisters too, and he didn't know that," she said, but while her words were serious, there was a little bit of humor on her face, and he took that as a good sign.

"In case you didn't notice, I'm not Ezra." He kind of held his breath after he said that, because that was something that was really important. He didn't want her to think of him as Ezra. He wanted her to know when she talked to him, she wasn't talking to Ezra. He wanted her to know who he was and like him for that, and not because of his family, or because of his brother.

"I've noticed." She looked down at her hands and then looked up, maybe a little reluctantly. The flickering flame of the kerosene light that he had lit when they first came in cast shadows across her face. But it didn't mar the beauty there. Nothing could. Not to him.

Her words gave him hope. She noticed that he wasn't his brother, and hopefully, that was a good thing to her. She opened her mouth to say more.

"I've noticed you're a lot less mature than he is."

Whoa. That wasn't what he wanted to hear. At least he didn't think so. Not being mature didn't really sound like a compliment. And that's what he was after, compliments. Or at least, an indication that he wasn't the little boy that she used to know. Or that when she looked at him, she saw someone who had grown up.

But no, she saw him as immature. Great. Maybe his plan would backfire, and she would hate him by the time they spent a week together. If they even got that far.

"That's not telling me what the problem is. I know you're not fine." He put his hands on the table and threaded them together. Holding them in front of him and keeping his eyes on her face, watching for expressions that told him how she felt, rather than words. Both seeing and hearing would give him a better picture.

"I'm just... I... I don't usually spend much time, you know, in silence. I have a TV, and it's on all the time. This quiet, this feeling of being the only people in the world is a little...a lot disconcerting. It doesn't help that my phone is completely dead."

"Do you think you might learn to like it?" He wasn't sure where that question came from, but he was curious. Sometimes when he came up, it was a bit of an adjustment for him to get used to the quiet of the cabin. Although, he was much more likely to start missing his brothers and sisters after a few days. But he noticed that if he allowed the feeling to pass, he really enjoyed the solitude. And he came back a better person because of it. He didn't think he could explain all of that to Sondra.

"I don't know. I... I feel anxious. Like, like I don't even know. I just want to scream almost, because it's too quiet. It's too...desolate here."

"Actually, it's not. Can I show you something?"

Her eyes flew to his, and he could see the fear that lurked there. "It's not too far? Is it outside the cabin?"

"We just need to step outside. We can leave the door open if you want to. Although, if we close it, it will keep the light from affecting what I want you to see."

"It has to be dark for me to see?"

"I think so."

He held a hand out, and she looked at it. Maybe she wondered whether or not she could trust him. Whether the little boy that she'd known, or the younger kid that she thought him to be, would be enough to protect her. Or maybe she just wasn't sure whether she could battle her own demons enough to leave this relative safety of the cabin.

Finally, she put those soft fingers into his, and he felt his mouth go dry.

He hadn't expected to have such a reaction to...was it her trust? Or maybe her touch. Maybe it was both. Whatever it was, he couldn't swallow.

He pushed back away from the table. "Come on. I think you're gonna like it."

He tugged on her hand, and she followed him to the door, where he opened it for her and she stepped out on the small porch he'd made. It was big enough for one chair. But there were two steps down to the ground, and he didn't bother with the chair but sat down on the top step, tugging on her hand to indicate he wanted her to sit down beside him.

He was pretty sure it was because of her fear that she sat so close. And not because she wanted to be near him.

Regardless, he liked the warmth he felt through his jeans and the companionship of having her beside him.

Maybe she didn't feel that way, but the same way that she made his grocery shopping memorable, she was making this night memorable as well. Although, he would be a lot happier if she didn't seem so afraid.

"Do you see that?" he asked, indicating the stars above them. He always noticed how the further he got into the mountains, the clearer the stars seemed to be. The lights of the city faded, and it allowed the stars to shine in all their glory.

"Yeah. They're stars."

She didn't sound impressed. He supposed if she didn't see it, the beauty and majesty he saw, he couldn't shove it down her throat.

"Listen," he said. The sounds of the night, the babbling brook down over the side of the mountain, some rustling in the leaves, either from wind or from an animal moving stealthily. The yapping of a few coyotes off in the distance, and perhaps that was a wolf howling far off.

"What are we listening for?" she asked.

"Well, there's things you don't hear, like cars, trains, even airplanes. You don't see too many of those in the sky here either."

"I'm supposed to be listening for the things I don't hear?"

"Do you hear the coyotes?"

She stilled. "Do they eat people?"

"No." As a general rule, what he just said was true, and he figured that now was not the time for him to go into the caveats that would make it untrue.

But her question took more of the wind out of his sails.

"There's something calming in nature. Something...that soothes you, relaxes you, and maybe puts you in awe of your creator. It's just...

You have to listen, you have to look, to see and smell. Do you hear the brook?"

"Oh. So is that what that sound is? Water is kind of relaxing." She said that casually, and he felt a little odd for the reverence that had been in his tone. But that's the way he felt when he listened to the night sounds, when he sat there on the porch, when he considered all the things that God had created, how amazing they all were. It was beautiful during the day, but he got that feeling of reverence at night.

"Can you smell anything?"

She sniffed, and then she said, "Is there a forest fire somewhere?"

He hadn't smelled any smoke. He breathed again. "No. I don't think so. It just smells like...the mountains at night in the spring. They have a different scent in the winter. And definitely a different scent in the fall. That's probably my favorite. They smell different in the summer too. They *feel* different in the summer as well. More alive, I think."

"That's so odd. You...smell the woods? Feel it?"

"Yeah. It's a lot different than the flatlands of North Dakota. Not better, just different. They have a smell all their own too, but it's not the same smell that you get up here. Like going to the ocean and smelling that."

"I've never been to the ocean."

"I was just there once. You can taste the salt in the air. That's a little different than here. I've never tasted anything."

She stuck her tongue out. "It just tastes like air to me." She shrugged her shoulders, and he laughed a little. She was being goofy, and that was better than being morose and sad, but she wasn't understanding what he was trying to show her.

"So is that what you do up here? You taste the air, smell it, and sit around and think about the stars?"

"Yeah. Pretty much. I have my Bible in there, and I read that a lot while I'm up here, too. I don't know how to explain it, but it feels like I'm closer to God when I'm up here. Not in a literal sense, like I went up the mountain, so I'm closer to the sky or whatever, but in a spiritual sense."

She had been being flippant, and he supposed he probably

shouldn't have said those things, because they were serious things, things that he didn't share with too many people, but he wanted to open up to her a little bit, because he knew that she was scared.

He wanted her to see that there wasn't anything to be scared about. That where they were was a beautiful place, with charm and blessing all its own, if they only opened up their senses to see it. Maybe it was more of a matter that God was speaking to them, showing off a little, and they just kept their eyes closed and didn't bother to pay attention to what God was doing. But He gave them beautiful things for their eyes, sweet melodies to listen to, and even attractive scents, ones that made him want to breathe deeply, which was probably good for his body, and God knew it and encouraged it.

He was also acutely aware that she had allowed her hand to stay in his. On one hand, he loved that and wanted to take care of her and to allay her fears.

On the other hand, he didn't want her to be driven to him because she was afraid and he was the only other human in a very long way that she could depend on.

There was a part of him that could get a power trip out of that, but that wasn't the way he wanted the relationship to be. He wanted her to fall for him because she saw him, not a protector or someone she could depend on. Although he wanted to be both of those things, and so much more.

"I guess this is your thing. But it definitely isn't mine." She wrapped her arms around her stomach, pulling her hand from his, and stood to her feet.

He felt cold and bereft, not just because he lost her warmth, but because he had hoped that she would share his deep love of God's creation and his admiration for the mountains, even though his heart would always be in North Dakota.

A gust of wind shook the trees and rattled something along the side of the cabin. He'd have to check that out tomorrow; something must be loose.

But for now, he stood with her.

"I didn't show you the bedroom, but it's just a small room through the only other door in the house. The outhouse is right over there." He nodded at the trail through the woods. It wasn't far away, although it didn't show in the circle of light.

"Oh my goodness," she breathed.

"Do you want me to walk you there?" He wanted to assure her that he'd been doing it for years and he'd never had a problem, but that probably wasn't going to make her feel any better.

Chapter Six

Taking Sondra to his cabin was a really horrendous idea. Asher should have just asked Tobias if he could have used his cabin for a little bit. Tobias lived on the ranch, but on the opposite side of their twenty-five thousand acres, and it was well enough away from everyone that he didn't have to run into anyone if he didn't want to.

But no, he'd decided to take her to his cabin in the mountains, eight hours from home. It would serve him right if she demanded to go home right away and he ended up driving all night to get her there. Which he would do, because it was the right thing to do. He had really given her no choice about going with him, and he didn't want her to be uncomfortable or petrified all night.

"Yeah. If you don't mind. I don't want to walk there by myself." She breathed out. "I hadn't given those people on the reality shows the credit they deserve. This is petrifying."

He chuckled but kept it quiet. She was still talking about her shows, which was okay, because that was part of who she was. It was just...funny. That out here, she could make the connection to Hollywood.

"Are you ready?"

"Is there...toilet paper out there?" she asked, almost reluctantly, like she was terribly afraid that he was going to say no, and she'd have to wipe with poison ivy leaves.

"Yeah. I make sure that I keep an entire package there. I'm pretty sure there's at least eight rolls."

"Oh. Okay." She looked visibly relieved.

"Are you coming?" He didn't move, waiting for her.

"Are you going to hold my hand?" she asked, and while he definitely didn't mind holding her hand, he was more than a little disappointed that she only wanted to hold his hand because she was scared.

He wasn't sure that fear was a great thing to build a relationship on, though he wasn't going to get nitpicky tonight.

"Of course." He held out his hand, waiting until she slid her fingers in it before he closed his around hers and held tight. "Are you ready?"

"I'd feel so much better if I had a flashlight. Even my phone flashlight would work."

"I do have a flashlight in the cabin, but I try to only use it for emergencies."

"Going to the bathroom in the dark is not an emergency?"

"No. I also have a bedpan inside, under the bed."

"A bedpan. I think I should know what that is, but...like an indoor toilet?" she said, hesitantly.

"I guess. Just something you can use if you can't make it to the outhouse. I... I did that once when I sprained both ankles. It was a little touch and go there for a bit, because walking was difficult. After a couple of days, I ended up crawling to the outhouse, because using a bedpan is gross. But to begin with, it was really nice to have."

"Who fed you?"

"I just ate cream cheese." He grinned down at her, and her serious expression froze for a minute as she processed his words, and then her face lifted up into a smile.

"You're a funny guy," she said as she bumped her shoulder into his. Well, she bumped her shoulder into his arm, since he was a good bit taller than she was, and the top of her head only came to his chin.

He hadn't really noticed their height difference, maybe because he never stood very close to her.

"I don't think anybody's ever accused me of that before," Asher said, and he realized it was true. He typically didn't say a whole lot, and when he did talk, it wasn't usually to crack a joke. At least, he didn't consider himself any funnier than the next guy, but he liked that Sondra seemed to think so.

Of course, he liked even more that he was able to get her to laugh. At least she wasn't looking like she was facing a night in the dungeon anymore.

They got to the outhouse, and he said, "Hang on a second. I'll open the door and go in. Just make sure that...everything's okay." He almost said, "to make sure no one made a home there while I was gone," but he didn't want to scare her. After all, he could tell her a couple of stories about finding animals in the outhouse. Including a snake. But he didn't want her to refuse to use it the entire time they were there.

She didn't question him but let go of his hand while he opened the door and stepped in.

It was pitch black inside, and he remembered that he had been thinking about replacing the roof with clear plastic. That would at least allow the sunlight in during the day, and if there was any moonlight at night to flow in, it wouldn't be quite so dark.

He had some spare batteries, and they should be fine for a week. Maybe he would see that she got the flashlight so she didn't have to go in the dark.

He looked around, made a bit of noise, made sure the seat was down so that she didn't end up sitting on the bare boards, and then walked back outside.

"Looks good. She's all yours."

"I'm not sure I'm going to be able to go with a man standing right outside the door."

"Okay. Do you want me to walk back to the cabin?" He was a little confused as to why that would make any difference, but maybe it was a woman thing. Since it certainly wouldn't bother him any if she stood outside.

"No," she said quickly. "I'll... I'll be okay. Just plug your ears."

"Right. Because... I have no idea what you're going in there to do, and we'd both be traumatized if I figured it out," he said, his eyes narrowed a little, as he tried to figure out if that was what she was thinking. Really, what difference would him covering his ears make?

"Okay. I understand what you're saying. I'm being ridiculous. But... humor me? I just don't think we know each other well enough for you to listen to me go to the bathroom."

"Sure.... I guess I didn't realize that was a stage in a relationship. Maybe you can enlighten me when we've reached that point."

"I am not going to stand here in the dark and talk about this. I already admitted I was being ridiculous. What else do you want me to say?"

"Nothing. Just go on in, and I will...feel like an idiot, but I'll cover my ears, okay?"

"Thank you," she said, huffing, like she just won a major victory after putting a whole pile of effort into it.

"My pleasure. Anytime I can look like an idiot for your benefit, I'm happy to oblige."

"You know, I would offer to stand outside and put my hands over my ears while you use this..." she hesitated, as though stumbling over what to call it, "...thing. But I am fairly certain that you don't particularly care whether I'm standing outside the door or not."

"I guess you're right... Sorry?"

She yanked the door open and stomped inside.

He laughed, and thought about how cute she was, and almost forgot to put his hands over his ears like he promised.

He really didn't see the point, but he was happy to do it if it made her happy. He supposed. Although, if there was anything looking at him right now, they would have to think that he was the most ridiculous human on the planet.

All for love.

He grew serious at the thought immediately. He hadn't really considered what he felt for Sondra to be love. He still didn't. Right? He just...had a little crush on her. His secret crush. Because she had been his brother's fiancée, and he could hardly let people know he was crushing on her.

Definitely, he was still crushing. But the more time he spent with her, the more he realized that they probably would never be able to be together. He thought the way she talked about her shows was cute, but he didn't really want to watch them with her, and that's probably what she would want. Someone who could enjoy the things that she enjoyed. Just the way it had been for her when he had sat her down on the porch, and she hadn't immediately seen everything that he had seen and felt when he sat there. He really, really liked her, but if they couldn't enjoy the same things, at least some of the same things, they couldn't be together.

Was he willing to buy a TV set just to be with her?

He supposed it wasn't that big of a deal. Everybody had TVs. But he couldn't imagine her determining that she was going to sit outside and learn to enjoy it, just for him. Right now, it wasn't too bad, but there would be mosquitoes later in the season, and that would drive even him inside.

"I'm done," Sondra said as she touched his elbow lightly.

He'd been so deep in thought, with his hands over his ears like he said, that he hadn't even heard her come out of the outhouse.

"All right," he said.

"That is nasty. In fact, I think that might be worse than being isolated in the middle of nowhere with no electronics and a dead phone."

"Wow. That bad?"

"Yes. There's no way to wash your hands."

"I actually have a container of antibacterial lotion at the cabin. I..." He was going to say that he didn't use it very often, but he didn't want to gross her out any more than what she already was. Honestly, he figured that a few germs were good for a person, although there came a point when it became unsanitary. Modern life was so far from that point though, it wasn't even funny. And modern medicine had proven the fact that exposure to germs made a person stronger. He didn't need to belabor that point.

"Oh. That's such a relief. I felt so icky."

"Yeah. No problem."

She hadn't noticed, at least not yet, that there was no washer and dryer, and she did not have a change of clothes. He had a few extra things in the cabin, but…they would be way too big for her. She might feel even more icky when she figured that out.

"Are you ready?" she asked, holding out her hand.

He grinned. "I'm starting to think you like me," he teased.

"I definitely like you whenever you're the only thing between me and…all of this darkness."

"Not the only thing. God is here."

She closed her mouth and looked away.

"Did I say something that offended you?" he asked low as they walked slowly back through the woods. The trail was well-worn, and he had made sure to keep it clear, but sticks fell all the time in the woods, sometimes whole tree limbs fell down. That wasn't uncommon, and more than once, he had to take his chainsaw out and clear the trail.

He'd always been grateful that he hadn't been walking on the trail when something fell. All joking aside, it would be a serious thing to be badly injured when he was this remote. He knew it, but…he still came up anyway.

"No not really. I believe in God and Jesus, I'm a Christian, but… I just never got the whole 'God is with you' thing. You know? We can't see Him, can't touch Him, He doesn't talk to you, and you can't hold His hand." She held up their joined hands.

"Well, God says He'll hold your right hand, that He'll comfort you." He knew God didn't mean it in a literal sense, but if God said He was going to do it, you could know that He was.

"Well, He's never done that for me."

"How do you know?"

She opened her mouth and then closed it again. It wasn't a question she could answer, and he enjoyed watching her face as she figured that out.

"I guess it's possible He has. But I've never known it."

"Sometimes maybe we don't know things, because we don't listen. We don't pay attention." He was thinking about when they'd been sitting on the porch and he'd been trying to get her to see and hear and smell what he could. She hadn't been able to, but it wasn't because the things weren't there. It was because she didn't want to listen, didn't want to see, didn't want to smell, didn't want to know.

"Are you still upset because I didn't like sitting on your porch?" she asked, and there was a little bit of teasing in her tone, but she didn't want to have a serious conversation about God.

He supposed that was up to her. The comfort was there, but a person had to accept it. It took faith. They had to believe. If they refused to believe, then...He couldn't help them. And God gave everyone free choice, so it was up to her. That made Asher sad. To think that Sondra would turn away from God, when He wanted so badly for her to know Him.

And turn to Him.

"Do I have to commit to a whole week here? Or are you willing to take me home if I want to go?"

They had reached the porch steps, and he put a hand on the banister. It was rough, made from lumber he'd hauled up and constructed himself.

He was a little proud of this cabin, because everything had been done by him. Maybe that was the reason that he offered to bring her to his cabin, rather than take her somewhere on Sweet View Ranch, which he loved.

It tore at his heart a little bit to think that she wanted to go home, but he certainly wasn't going to make her stay if she didn't want to.

"No. You don't. And yes, I will."

She laughed that he'd answered both questions.

"Do you want to go now?" He shoved a hand in his pocket, balling his fingers into a fist and waiting on her answer. He didn't want to ask the question, didn't want to make the offer, didn't want to leave.

"No. I'll stay. I... Actually... Tomorrow, can we go home please?"

"Yeah. I'm sorry. I shouldn't have brought you."

She didn't say anything, which made him feel even worse.

Finally he said, "Let me show you where the flashlight is, and I'll give it to you for tonight. I should have gone out tonight and cut some wood, but I'll do that first thing in the morning, so if I'm not in the cabin when you get up, that's where I'll be, okay?"

He didn't want her to be any more scared than what she needed to be.

"Even though we're not going to stay, I like to have a little stash that's ready so I can use it when I get here, in case I come like we did tonight. I'll get a fire started, because it will be pretty chilly tonight. You'll feel the heat through the walls, and the stovepipe goes up through your room. You should be toasty."

"What about you?" It was like she hadn't considered that there was only one room until just that second. "Where are you going to sleep?"

"I've slept outside before. I might do that. I have a couple of blankets in the toolbox of my pickup. I've slept on the back of my truck when I was building the cabin and sometimes afterward, just because I love it. The stars are really pretty, and sometimes I brought Jack up, he kept me warm." He referred to the dog they used to have, and she laughed. Remembering.

"He was such a joker. I've never seen a funnier dog, but he loved your family."

"Yeah. He did. We loved him." So much that even though they had gotten another dog since him, Jack held a special place in his heart.

"All right. Show me where that flashlight is, because I'm tired."

He didn't think she really wanted to go to bed, but he was pretty sure she didn't want to stand outside, because it made her nervous. Some people just weren't meant to be outdoors, especially at night.

Without saying anything else, he went in, got the flashlight for her, showed her her bedroom, and told her that he had just put fresh sheets on it, because he had taken the other sheets home to wash them last time he was there. That's when another light dawned in her eyes.

"There's no washer or dryer here, is there?"

He grinned. "If I have to wash something, I do it at the creek. Although, I also take things home, obviously."

"Well. I don't even have a change of clothes. I couldn't stay for a week. There is no way. Plus, I am...more anxious without my phone than I expected."

"I understand."

"I don't think you do," she said, and with that, she walked to the door of the bedroom, putting her hand on it and waiting for him to walk through before she closed it behind him.

He supposed that was his clue that he was dismissed. This entire thing had been a dismal failure, and he'd be taking her home first thing in the morning. He couldn't deny he was disappointed.

Chapter Seven

Sondra's eyes flew wide open. Where was she? What was she doing? What was that strange smell? And why was she...in a bed that wasn't hers?

She sat bolt upright before she remembered everything about last night.

The sun was up, shining brightly, and vaguely she realized that there had been some kind of crash that had woken her.

Something out in the woods. Hopefully it wasn't a bear.

Asher had said something about getting firewood, so maybe he... chopped a tree down or something?

She wasn't sure, but she did know that it was cold, and she was tempted to lie back down and snuggle under the blankets, but the bed wasn't exactly the kind of bed she wanted to snuggle in.

It wasn't uncomfortable. In fact, she'd gone to sleep far easier than she ever thought she would, especially since there was no TV to keep her company. She'd lain down, sunk deep into the mattress, and with the heavy blanket on top of her, she felt almost like she was in some kind of cocoon, safe and warm and wrapped up tight.

She closed her eyes and hadn't awoken until just then.

But there was just something off about the cabin. It was so...rustic.

Just not her type of thing at all. She realized that she enjoyed watching reality shows where people suffered in outdoorsy-type conditions, but experiencing them was something completely different. She'd stick to TV from now on. She had all she wanted of the camping life.

If that's what this even was. Camping was probably worse.

She was starving, and she remembered all the cream cheese that they had in the refrigerator. He'd also gotten eggs and bread, milk and... She felt bad that he'd have to haul all those groceries back to Sweet Water. If he even did that. It was probably cold enough that they would stay fresh in the back of his truck... She wasn't sure. She didn't haul groceries across state lines as a general rule, and she had no idea how long they would stay good. She'd feel bad, if she found out they were going to lose it all, but that didn't make her want to stay. Not even a little. She definitely wanted to get out of here and the sooner the better.

Asher hadn't talked to her last night about who was going to cook, but first she had to take care of something else.

The dreaded outhouse.

Maybe she could use the bedpan. That would be far more preferable to going to the outhouse again. It had been so creepy, and the hole as black as pitch. She couldn't tell if there was anything in there or not, and to put her bare body over top of it... It took an extreme amount of willpower. Thankfully, nothing had eaten her, and she hadn't even had something try to take a bite of her. She considered that a win for survival and didn't intend to go back.

So, the bedpan was much better, and she used it without too much trouble. Then, she realized that someone had to empty it.

Deciding that she'd deal with that later, she set it aside and got dressed.

She still didn't hear any sound that might be Asher as she squirted some antibacterial gel on her hands and rubbed it in before opening the door to the bedroom and walking out.

"Asher?" she called, looking around the kitchen, but it was totally empty.

It didn't look like he had had any breakfast, since there were no plates in the sink, so she decided that she might as well do it. And then she realized there was no stove.

He had mentioned the night before about starting a fire in the woodstove. And it did feel warm in the kitchen. Warmer than her bedroom.

She went over and peered at it. She could see a little orange glow through one of the knobs and decided that he must have indeed started a fire. Maybe he was outside cutting more wood. Or splitting it or chopping it or whatever it was that he did with wood.

She liked it much better when she could just flip the thermostat on and have heat.

She wouldn't need to worry about a fire keeping her warm, ever again. It wasn't something she thought about in her life before, and she had no intention of worrying about it after she left today. Hopefully soon.

As soon as Asher was ready to take her, they were going home.

At least she knew he was going to take her. He wasn't going to make her stay in this creepy cabin in the middle of nowhere, with no electricity, no running water, no toilet for goodness' sake, for days on end.

Maybe he'd even take her straight to Wyoming. Back to her house, although the idea of that made her sad. She had missed the Clybourns since they'd left and had been looking forward to seeing them again. She wouldn't consider them great friends, but she did consider them friends.

Unsure as to whether or not the stove was hot enough to cook on, she figured it was all she had, she might as well use it. Or at least attempt to use it.

She'd cooked plenty of times herself, even though she'd taken to eating more salads and that type of thing, but it was easy to fry bacon and eggs, and she figured she might as well use some of the cream cheese they'd gotten, so she threw it in the eggs, unsure of how it would taste, but if it was terrible, she could at least remind Asher that he had said cream cheese made everything better.

Regardless, she was able to get the stove to work, and while there wasn't an overabundance of utensils, she had the eggs ready and the bacon frying, and Asher still hadn't appeared.

She had reached for her phone at least seven times to text him and ask where he was. She had reached for her phone even more just to check it, because she wasn't used to getting up in the morning without looking at her social media accounts. She didn't even cook without something playing in the background, the TV, for sure, and sometimes something on her phone as well. The silence was unnerving.

It had surprised her that she'd even been able to go to bed last night as quiet as everything was. Normally she had the TV on while she slept.

After she was done cooking, with the food sitting on the table getting cold, the silence pushing in on her, the fear that always felt like it was right at the back of her mind came trickling out.

She tried to tell herself it was fine. Asher was here, she was not alone, and everything was going to be fine.

As she thought that, she saw the Bible that he'd talked about sitting on the windowsill right by the door.

He must grab it on his way out to sit on the porch and read. Maybe he'd already read it that morning.

She knew Ezra had that habit, the one of reading the Bible every day. That was a little bit more of a dedicated Christian than what she wanted to be. She just wanted fire insurance, something to keep her out of hell, but she didn't want to actually change her life and start living in a different way. That was too radical. Not to mention, she liked her life. She liked her shows, movies, and social media that kept her busy. She even liked her job, although she put her eight hours in and was done.

She didn't want to change. She didn't want to become a radicalized Christian, who actually...lived Bible principles or whatever it was. Whatever it was that made Christians weird and different. She wanted to blend in with the crowd and be a part of that.

Still, for some reason her gaze remained caught on the Bible.

She smiled, thinking of Asher reading it. If he loved it as much as Ezra did, it was precious to him.

She looked back at the table at the food that was now cold.

She should have waited until she knew for sure that he was coming before she started to cook. Surely... Surely he would have known that she would be getting up, and would come to check on her? She couldn't tell what time it was. There was a clock in the kitchen, but it was stopped. And she didn't have her phone. But the sun was well up in the sky, and it felt late. Her stomach growled.

Maybe she should eat without him. That would serve him right, for not being here when he knew that she would be getting up and wondering where he was.

But part of her said that Asher was considerate. He'd been considerate with every single thing that he'd done. He hadn't even taken her away without asking her permission first. He wouldn't all of the sudden change, would he?

Maybe he was upset because she had said that she wanted to go home. She supposed that was a possibility.

But he hadn't seemed upset last night. He agreed immediately when she said that she wanted to go home. He hadn't tried to argue with her or convince her to stay. He'd just accepted the fact that she just wasn't a mountain girl.

Or a roughing-it girl, or an outhouse kind of girl. That was disgusting. The less she thought about the outhouse, the better.

She stood up, pacing around the room, which felt small.

Finally, she went in and made her bed, thinking she would pack up her things, except...she didn't have any things.

Everything that she had, she had on, except for her shoes. She put those on and walked to the door. Looking out.

Asher was nowhere in sight.

She thought about the crash she heard when she had woken up. She had been too busy to think about it again, but...what if it wasn't a normal kind of crash?

That was not a thought she wanted to think, but she put her hand on the doorknob and turned, opening it and stepping out.

The fear that had been slithering around inside of her head burst into flames. She took a deep breath.

"Asher?" she called into the woods, but nothing answered her. It felt like a big, silent void, but she could remember Asher yesterday saying to listen. That if she listened, she could hear things that maybe she didn't pay attention to. And sure enough, she heard the bubbling of the creek.

Would he be down there? If he were, he probably couldn't hear her. But would he have stayed down there for as long as it took her to get up, cook breakfast, for breakfast to get cold, and for her to come outside?

She was pretty sure not.

"Asher?" she said again, this time louder.

There was still silence. The bubbling of the creek was there, but it didn't sound comforting. He said it was relaxing, but it just said "fear" to her.

"Asher!" She screamed this time. Still nothing.

She glanced around the clearing, wondering where in the world he would have gone to get the firewood. That's what he said he was going to do this morning. He had to be somewhere. Had to be. He wouldn't have left her here alone. That was a dirty joke and not something that Asher would do. Maybe Tobias would have. Although he wouldn't have been nearly as friendly or nice. He would have abducted her without saying anything, dropped her off in the middle of nowhere, and laughed the whole way home about it.

That wasn't true. Tobias wasn't mean, but he was quiet, and he was probably the Clybourn that she knew the least about. Still, the fact of the matter was, this was not something that Asher would do for a joke.

For the first time, she wondered if...he was hurt.

He hadn't mentioned bears, but surely there were bears, cougars, and all kinds of animals that could hurt a person running around in the woods.

He hadn't been scared last night, hadn't taken any weapon that she could see to the outhouse with them even in the dark. He hadn't even taken a light. Did that mean there was nothing to be afraid of? Or did that mean he was foolish and hadn't taken the proper precautions, and now he'd been eaten by a wild animal, and she was alone in the woods.

How long should she wait for him to come back before she got in his truck and left?

Could she even drive his truck?

It was a lot bigger than her car, and she didn't know where the keys were. She remembered seeing him taking them out of the ignition last night, and she did notice that he hadn't locked it. She'd laughed to herself at the time, thinking that what, was a bear going to hop in the truck and take it somewhere?

But where and what had he done with the keys?

And if he was going to leave her, wouldn't he have taken the truck?

Could she leave without finding him at least?

She had to be brave. Although she didn't feel the slightest bit brave.

The LORD is my strength and my shield; my heart trusted in him.

She didn't know where that verse had come from, but she clung to it. And then, she made a deal with God, "If you help me find Asher, I'll read that Bible."

Chapter Eight

S ondra took one step down, and then she turned back and ran inside the cabin.

She was not going to go out without a weapon. She wasn't a big believer in guns. She did understand that they were needed for self-defense, and she also understood the reason there was a Second Amendment in the Constitution. It didn't take a lot of brainpower to see the colonists had needed to fight their own government in order for them to be free.

She didn't expect that to happen in her lifetime, but she understood that if a people were not armed, the government could get away with whatever they wanted to. Still, the idea of using guns to get her way, even to fight, wasn't something that she was interested in. Even though she realized at times in history it had been necessary.

Nonetheless, at that moment, she wished she had one. She'd feel a lot safer. Even though she didn't know how to use one, it would still make her feel better.

Regardless, she looked around the kitchen, trying to figure out what she could use instead. There weren't too many drawers—just two. She opened one. There was silverware and a few measuring spoons; it was sparse.

Nothing she could use.

She opened the next one, and bingo. Knives.

There were three, a small knife that she might use for paring fruit or potatoes, a larger knife that might be a steak knife, and a long, wicked-looking knife that probably was for chopping vegetables.

She really was tempted to take the biggest knife. The bigger the knife, the bigger the protection, right? But she didn't think she'd be able to wield something like that, so she put her fingers around the smallest knife and picked it up.

Could she kill something with this?

That was probably a stupid question. She figured if she were fighting for her life, she could do whatever it took. Until that point in time, where her life was on the line, she would remain a pacifist.

She supposed that made her a circumstantial pacifist.

So be it. Normal people weren't afraid to fight for their lives if necessary. Right?

She wasn't sure. This type of thing didn't happen in any of her reality TV shows.

At that thought, she remembered the few thriller movies she'd watched. Could there be a stalker in the woods? Was there some kind of human walking around, who attacked Asher, and now he was waiting to attack her.?

Her heart thumped against her ribs, and her stomach seemed to search for a way out. She eyed the bigger knife again, wishing she had the bravery to take it out, knowing it would most likely be knocked out of her hand, but there were no rules that said she couldn't take two knives, so she went ahead and grabbed the big knife and held that in her left hand. Keeping the small knife in her dominant hand.

Feeling a bit like he-woman, but still so scared her knees knocked together, she put the big knife between her teeth so she could open the door.

She would be laughing at herself if she weren't so scared. Scared for herself, but petrified for Asher as well. Something had happened to him. Why wasn't he back?

The LORD is my strength and my shield; my heart trusted in him.

She said the verse again, realizing as she did so that repeating it gave her comfort. She thought, although she wasn't sure, that David had written the psalms, at least some of them, when he was in some kind of battle. Possibly he was scared as well. Maybe he'd written those words so that he would feel better, and down through the ages, they made her feel better as well.

She thought about all the different times those words had been quoted by Christians facing difficult things and trying hard not to be scared, just as she was at that point.

There were a lot of people who had been in her shoes, maybe not exactly in a cabin in the woods looking for the friend who had brought them there, but who were so scared they could barely think straight and they clung to that verse, and that was a comfort in itself.

Stepping off the porch, she scanned around the clearing again. Seeing nothing.

What was he wearing? She couldn't even remember. Something blue, maybe.

She looked for a glimpse of blue. Was he lying in a heap on the ground somewhere? There wasn't that much cleared area, but the grass had grown up, and a body could have fallen down and be partially hidden.

She walked out a little more, keeping an eye out for bears and cougars and lions and elephants or whatever might be in the woods. She didn't even know. She didn't care, she just wanted to go home!

She had to find Asher, first. She could hardly leave without him.

A part of her said: she couldn't leave until she knew whether he was alive...or dead.

Dead. That was a word she didn't want to think about again.

Swallowing hard, her breath coming in short, shallow gasps, and her heart pounding so hard she felt it in her toes, she made herself walk forward. She couldn't remember ever being more scared in her life before, but she had to find Asher. _She had to._

Her eyes scanned the perimeter of the property again, expecting to see some kind of wild animal jumping out at any minute. Then, she remembered something about panthers and trees. Her eyes jerked up, looking to see if there was any danger lurking in any branches.

The trees blew lazily in the breeze, and to her surprise, the sky beyond was blue. The sun shone, puffy white clouds floated across the sky, and it seemed surreal. Shouldn't there be thunderclouds? Lightning? Dark, evil breezes, and weird sounds?

That's the way it would be in movies anyway.

White puffy clouds didn't really dispel any fear, it just made it seem weird that things could feel so normal, when everything was so not normal in her life.

"Asher?" she said, her voice barely a whisper.

If there was someone lurking around the trees, waiting to grab her too, she didn't want to alert them to the fact that she was out of the safety of the cabin.

The cabin was safe, wasn't it?

She didn't even want to think that.

Lord, I'm petrified. So petrified that I don't even know if I can function.

She took some more gasping breaths. She had to get a hold of herself. If she was going to die, she would die and it would be over. But being this petrified was so miserable she almost wished she could die.

Lord, help me find Asher. Please.

She took three more steps and was halfway through the clearing.

"Asher?"

Nothing. Not a sound, other than the creek and leaves and her own labored breathing. Maybe there were some birds chirping too. She had no idea what kind they were, and...she didn't care, as long as they weren't man-eating birds. Or scared-woman-eating birds.

Holding tight to both knives, she told herself, "I am brave. I am strong. I will find Asher."

She laughed. Who was she kidding?

She was petrified, she was weak, and she didn't have any hope of ever —what was that?

She blinked, was that blue in the woods?

She moved her head a little, and it disappeared.

It looked like something blue, maybe lying on what looked like might be a trail going off into the woods.

Would he have a trail where he was going to get wood?

She didn't know how to tell, but she supposed the grass did look like it was tramped down a little there. Maybe he had been out there this morning.

That was him. What else would be blue in the woods?

She had no idea. Was there some kind of man-eating animal that was blue? Bears? Weren't they black? Or brown? Or...grizzled? No, please no. Not grizzled bears. She really didn't think her knife was going to do much good against a bear of any caliber, but definitely not a grizzly bear. She was pretty sure, even though the cabin wasn't that far away, she wasn't going to outrun anything. She should have lost the extra thirty pounds she carried around her waist.

Even then, she wouldn't have a hope of outrunning a bear.

Stop thinking about bears!

She looked again, trying to see the blue thing again. Taking a few steps forward, while looking all around, knives at the ready.

In the back of her head, she knew that if anyone had been filming her, she would have made a viral TokBok video by now. Not because she was so compelling, but because she was so ridiculous.

Still, until someone was out in the woods by themselves, possibly being stalked by a serial killer or some kind of wild, man-eating animal, they didn't know what fear was.

They would be doing the same thing.

She told herself that anyway, although it didn't really make her feel any better. Still, she needed something to occupy her mind as the blue thing appeared and disappeared as the leaves shifted.

She had to get closer. It could be a trap, a trap set by whatever serial killer was stalking her, but it could also be Asher. Although she hoped not, because it wasn't moving. And he obviously didn't hear her. And that didn't bode well at all.

Chapter Nine

Sondra crept forward quietly, knives at the ready, eyes scanning everywhere. She took another four steps, and the woods opened up enough that she could tell that yes, indeed, the thing that she had seen was a flannel shirt. The blue flannel shirt Asher had been wearing yesterday and still wore today. It would make sense; he probably didn't have any clothes either. Although, there had been a small dresser in her room. She hadn't even bothered to look at it, but he hadn't come in to get any clothes, so he would have been stuck wearing whatever he wore yesterday.

She swallowed, looking around again, moving closer. And that's when she realized what the problem was.

The knives slowly lowered, and she hurried forward. Careful not to fall, knowing that if she did so, she was just as likely to stab herself as she was to do anything.

A big, twisted tree branch had fallen down and now lay on top of Asher. His form was still, although she thought she saw blood on his temple.

She couldn't tell, because he was mostly facing away from her. But she couldn't deny that on one hand, she felt relief. There was no serial killer. At least, not one that had gotten Asher. And no wild animal. None so far anyway. It was a tree branch.

Slowly she began to realize that maybe they were still in danger. Maybe there were more tree branches that would fall down?

But it didn't matter, she had to figure out first of all, was he alive?

Then, after she figured that out...

One step at a time. Just do one thing. The next thing. Just do the next thing. Don't think about the big picture.

She liked to know everything, have all the details, get everything organized so she could look at it all, but that was too overwhelming right now. She could just do one thing, and that was to figure out whether or not Asher was still alive.

She crept closer, dropping the knives and moving around the mangled tree branch, trying not to touch it at all, because she didn't want it to shift on Asher and hurt him more, if he was still alive.

Although, the way it was lying on him, she wasn't sure if he'd be able to breathe or not.

Lord. Let him be alive. Please?

She wasn't much of a praying person, but today had seemed like a really good time to start.

She'd already made a deal with God, and He helped her find Asher. Maybe, maybe He would give her another answer to her prayer and let Asher be alive.

She was able to kneel down beside him, and her fingers slid around his neck, searching for the pulse that was supposed to be there.

She couldn't remember ever before in her life checking to see if a person was alive or not, and so, it wasn't surprising that it took a while.

His skin was warm. That was a good sign, wasn't it?

She moved her fingers. Still nothing.

She moved them again. *Come on. There's a heartbeat in there somewhere. There has to be.*

The fear that wasn't exploded in her brain traveled down her torso and out her fingers and toes, making her want to scream and run. Run away. Run somewhere safe, but where? Where was safe?

Every place was scary.

She took another breath. Deep breaths seemed to calm her a little bit, and she adjusted her fingers yet again.

Please. Lord. Please. She found herself chanting, begging God to let her find a pulse.

She didn't find a pulse, but Asher groaned. Just a small sound, almost indiscernible, but she heard it. He moved just a bit. She felt relief flooding through her, cool and so very, very welcome.

He was alive!

That made everything shift and change, just because...she wasn't alone anymore.

"Asher?" she said, putting her hand on his shoulder and shaking gently.

There was no response. Not even a groan.

Looking more closely, she could see that there was still blood seeping out of the wound in his temple. She had no idea what other injuries he might have, but she seemed to recall that there was some kind of protocol about not moving a person in case they had a back injury.

But... Maybe there were certain instances where she wouldn't follow that protocol. For example, when a person was completely alone in the middle of the woods with no way of contacting the outside world, no cell phone, no electricity, she didn't even know where the key to the pickup was. She had to get him out of the woods. And someone would have to go somewhere to contact someone, but she couldn't just leave him here.

She stood, putting her arms around her stomach and bending over, hating the way her entire body seemed to be tight and electrified with fear.

How could she help him? Should she leave him, try to go get help? Or at least try to go somewhere where she could make a phone call?

She tried to think of how far away he had said the closest store was. Wasn't it an hour? Something like that. She didn't even know if she could drive his truck. It was a lot bigger than her car, and she still didn't know where the keys were.

He was going to die, just because she had no idea what to do, and it was going to be all her fault, she would have to live with this for the rest of her life, and she would have to explain to his siblings what she had done, and how incompetent she was—

She tried to get a hold of herself. She couldn't allow her mind to run away like that. She had to focus. Only a few seconds had gone by, but it seemed like an eternity while she stood there, trying to figure out what to do, panicking over outcomes that hadn't even happened yet.

Lord? I already owe You. I know. Because You answered my last two prayers. But I feel like I can't do this on my own, and...You are all I have.

She didn't quite think God was going to appreciate her saying that He was her last hope. She supposed He probably wanted to be her first hope.

She wasn't quite sure where she heard the phrase, but "do it afraid" came into her head.

Do it afraid.

She was scared, she didn't know what to do, and she was afraid she would do the wrong thing. But doing nothing would be worse than doing something wrong.

The first thing she needed to do was decide whether she was going to leave him there while she went for help or work on getting him in the cabin. Which seemed like an impossible task, especially if he didn't wake up.

She tried to weigh the pros and cons, trying to be analytical about the situation, but the only thing she could come up with was...she couldn't drive. That obstacle seemed too big to overcome, even bigger than the obstacle of trying to get Asher from where he was to inside his cabin.

"All right. I'm going to work on getting you in the cabin. I'm not going to think about leaving again. Not until you're inside anyway."

She might try to revisit things at that point, but she was making a decision and was going to stick to it. A decision that could potentially hurt him, since she was going to move him without knowing whether or not he had a back injury.

But she had to do something, and...that was the decision she was going to make, and she wasn't going to continuously second-guess herself, or she'd never get anything done.

Scared, her hands shaking, she knew the first thing she had to do was get the branch off of him, so she tried to lift it up.

It was too heavy.

It wouldn't roll. She could tell that right away, since there were branches sticking out of it, and it sat at an awkward angle across Asher's back.

What now?

She felt like she needed to move him as soon as possible.

She looked around, seeing a chainsaw, and some things lying beside it, over by a tree, possibly where Asher had been standing when he had been hit by the dead branch.

She walked over, knowing she had no idea how to use a chainsaw, so while that would seem like the easiest solution, it wasn't going to work for her. She could probably pull the chain, but once she had it started, what would she do? Just put it on the branch? Wouldn't that apply pressure to Asher and make things worse?

There was a wedge and also an ax or hatchet type of thing.

She looked at that for a moment and then wondered if she could stick the wedge underneath the tree and use the hatchet to pound it further in, not lifting the branch off him completely but getting it up far enough that she could slide him out.

That was something she could try, at least, so she grabbed the wedge, shocked at how heavy it was, and ended up using two hands to carry it back, looking for a point where she could shove it under the branch that would lift it up off him after she started hitting it with the hatchet.

She found a spot she thought would work, although she knew she wasn't going to get much room. Maybe an inch. That might be a bit of an overestimation.

Regardless, she hurried back over, tramping through the brush and briars, scratching herself but barely noticing it, as she grabbed the ax and hurried back.

She had no idea what she was going to do with Asher when she got him out, if she got him out, but it seemed like it was important to at least try and do it fast. As long as it didn't cause her to make a mistake, she figured it would be okay. She could do this.

God was with her.

She paused at that thought. It really did make her feel better. Like she wasn't...alone.

Kneeling down beside the wedge and backing up a little to give herself some room to swing it, she checked to make sure she wasn't going to hit Asher, then moved her angle just a bit. That would be a little hard to explain. How she managed to kill an unconscious man with an ax on accident.

She swung the ax and missed the wedge, hitting the tree.

Well. Okay. That was a practice swing.

She tried again, and the ax glanced off the edge of the wedge, but she was heartened that the wedge moved just a bit.

It dug into the ground anyway. She wasn't sure whether she was lifting the branch off at all, but even a half an inch would give her enough room to start pulling and ease the pressure off Asher.

She swung again, and that time, it was a solid blow. The wedge moved, and the branch...maybe it lifted. She tried a couple more times, hitting the branch twice more and totally missing everything on one blow, swiping at air.

But it didn't matter. Even if one blow out of ten hit the wedge, eventually she'd have it under the tree if she didn't give up.

Finally, she thought she might have it high enough, so she set the ax down and scooted over to Asher. She smiled, even though she was still petrified. It had worked! She could see already that the point where the branch had been lying on top of Asher was now sticking a little bit in the air. Just to be sure, she ran her hand down Asher's chest and ran it right under the branch.

Mission accomplished.

Well, the first part of the mission. She had a lot more mission to go. Now, all she had to do was figure out how she was going to get Asher out from underneath the branch, and into the cabin, and preferably in bed.

She took a deep breath, blew it out. The only thing she knew to do was to stick her arms underneath both of his armpits and pull. But if he had any type of injury, if the branch had broken ribs or given him any kind of internal damage, surely pulling him like that would make it worse?

She felt like she didn't have a choice.

Bending down, she tried to figure out how to get her arms underneath his. It was an awkward angle, to try to lift him up and shove her arms under him at the same time.

Less desirable would be to grab one of his arms and pull, which she hated to do, because that seemed like it would hurt even worse, but she didn't think she was going to have a choice.

Deciding that getting him out of the woods was more important than worrying about whether or not she aggravated his injuries, she quit trying to figure out how to lift his torso to get her arms underneath it and just grabbed his right arm, since the branch had landed on his left, and tried to pull.

That elicited a groan out of him. She assumed that meant it hurt.

"Asher?" she asked, hopeful that he had least woken up.

But he didn't answer. Didn't move, didn't respond at all.

She tried not to be discouraged. She'd already figured out that he was heavy, a lot heavier than what she was expecting, and pulling him out was not going to be easy. Plus, there were a lot of brambles and briars and that type of thing around her, and it was going to hurt. Both of them.

But the little bit of pain she was going to go through seemed to be nothing compared to what he had, so...she picked up his arm and pulled again.

This time, his groan was louder, and it ended abruptly, but he didn't open his eyes or respond when she said his name, although she didn't stop pulling. She couldn't stop pulling every time he groaned, or she'd never get anything done.

Even though those groans made her feel like she was hurting him, and she wanted to stop. Wanted to apologize, at the very least. It was foolish to apologize to a man who couldn't hear her. Plus, she was pretty sure she was doing him a favor.

Chapter Ten

Taking hold of Asher's hand with both of hers, Sondra set her feet on the ground and pulled with all her might. He moved probably three inches.

But that was three inches closer to the cabin. She tried to encourage herself.

Come on, three more inches. Setting her feet again, she pulled as hard as she could.

She hadn't realized her hands were sweating until they slipped off his, and she went rushing backward, slamming her side against a tree and falling to the ground, right in the middle of a briar patch.

It hurt. A lot. That's when she looked down and realized her arms were bleeding, scratched from the briars she'd already been through and barely noticed. But there was definitely a thorn stuck in her rear, one in her thigh, and one had scratched along the bottom of her rib cage. She figured by the time she managed to get herself up, she'd have them sticking out of other places as well.

But there wasn't anyone to help her out, and until she got up, there was no one to help Asher. So, trying to ignore the pain, she pushed herself forward, briars digging into her arm, shoulder, and the one in her rear pushing deeper, as she adjusted her legs to get them underneath her to push up.

The briars made a tearing sound on her clothing as she pulled away from them, ripping and struggling.

She might have been able to pick just one branch of briars off her, but this was an entire bush. Or whatever it was, they looked like canes sticking up out of the ground.

Finally she was free and hurried back over to Asher. She had about four feet to pull him before she got on the trail. After that, it might not be easier, he would still be just as heavy as he was right now, but at least she wouldn't be pulling him over rocks and through briars.

"I'm sorry. I know this hurts. It hurts me too," she said, feeling better if she were talking, as she grabbed his hands and made sure her grip on him was firm before she started tugging.

She grunted and said, "It looks a lot easier on TV. In fact, it looks a lot different on TV."

Another three inches. She backed her feet up a bit, set them, and pulled again. "In fact, I would say that TV is totally fake. You absolutely do not understand how scared people are when they're in the woods by themselves, alone, with nothing. TV does not show that to you."

She was kind of working up a little bit of anger toward the false advertising that TV shows obviously did, and maybe that was a good thing, because she'd managed to move him almost a foot. It made her a little nervous though, because the branch was now over top of his stomach, and if it fell again, if it didn't hold, it could do some serious damage.

Not that it hadn't already. She looked at his head. It was still seeping blood, but not gushing. Maybe she should have tried to stop the bleeding before she got him out.

There had been a lot of blood lost already, if the dark red pool beside where his head had been was any indication.

She heard that head wounds bled a lot, and so she hoped that was all there was to it.

Regardless, she'd already decided to get him out from underneath the tree, and that's what she would do. So, she dug her feet in and continued to pull, thinking ahead about how if she were making a TV show, she wouldn't want to do it wrong. She would want to make sure that it was as accurate as possible. After all, people like her believed that kind of stuff. And yet, here she was, realizing that most of what she'd seen had to have been fake.

Finally, it felt like forever, but she had all but his feet out from underneath the branch. She needed to let go of him and twist his feet a little, because they weren't going to fit. She adjusted his legs so that his feet fell outward, and after eyeing the log, she decided that there would be enough room for them to slip through. Hopefully.

She wanted to celebrate her victory, the victory of at least getting Asher out from underneath the log, but she was so concerned that she was hurting him that she just didn't feel celebration was in order.

A few more tugs, and he was completely out and his head and shoulders were on the trail.

She was going to have to turn him a little to get him completely on it and headed toward the cabin.

Not that the trail was well beaten, it was just...cleared off.

"Asher?" she said, coming around and kneeling beside him. Looking at the wound which still oozed thick, red blood.

She looked around for something to press against it. Maybe she should try cleaning it off and looking to see how deep it was, but it wasn't going to matter. She couldn't change the way she treated it whether it was a half an inch deep or just a surface scratch.

It might need stitches, but she definitely didn't know how to do that. And didn't have the equipment for it anyway. She'd need a needle at the very least. And she wasn't exactly someone who sewed or carried a needle and thread around with her wherever she went.

No, it was going to have to be okay until they got to the cabin. She might be able to clean it off a little bit to put a bandage over top of it and maybe kinda try to pull the two ends of skin together with the bandage. She could kind of picture doing that in her head.

And she thought she might have seen that on TV too.

Maybe there were some benefits to TV, although she felt a little skeptical, since they had gotten the whole thing about being alone in the woods all wrong.

She didn't see anything she could press against it, and so she grabbed a hold of his arm and pulled again. He groaned occasionally, and she didn't even stop pulling. "We have to get you to the cabin."

He didn't answer her, not that she expected him to. But it did make her feel better to talk to him.

"It's too bad your feet couldn't have been pointed toward the cabin. I think it would be a lot easier to pick up both of those and haul you that way. It might even be better for you. Might hurt less anyway. Although, I think whatever I do is going to hurt. I'm not sure exactly what you did, but...it's a doozy."

What if she hadn't been there?

He had been at the cabin a lot by himself, and he'd chopped wood, and...had he even made the cabin himself? She hadn't thought to ask, but she thought he'd mentioned it. She'd been kind of wrapped up in herself and her own fear. Fear was still there, but the idea of Asher in the woods alone, without anyone to help him, unconscious, made her shiver. He could have died out here, and no one would have known it for...days.

She didn't know if he was even checking in with his family. They might not expect to hear from him for days or a week. Or more.

Surely he had a cell phone somewhere. When she had said hers was dead, he hadn't said anything, but she hadn't seen it at all. Not on the ride there, not after they got there. If he had one, she had no idea where it was.

By that time, she'd managed to pull him to the edge of the woods. Now all she had to do was pull him to the cabin, then somehow, she had to figure out how to get him up the steps.

It was too bad he didn't have a wheelbarrow or something she could use. Although that wouldn't help her with the steps.

But she did think it would be easier to pull his legs.

She took a break, standing up and straightening her back, feeling the kinks and the soreness settle in the lower part. She put her hands on it and stretched.

She was almost halfway there.

She looked from the cabin back to Asher. Would it be faster to pull him by his legs?

Twisting him around was probably going to hurt him, and she decided to just finish the job the way she started.

He hadn't woken up by the time she managed to get him over to the steps, and it was a difficult job to get him up the steps. Using both arms to lift his head and shoulders, she basically sat behind him, putting her arms underneath his armpits and scooting her butt up the stairs. If any kind of doctor or emergency personnel could see what she was doing, they would probably have a heart attack on the spot.

She just hoped she wasn't making things worse, though she had a feeling she was, but still, what was she going to do? Leave him out in the yard?

She fought with the guilt, and it almost overtook the fear.

But finally she managed to get him in the house. She was dirty, bloodied, sore, exhausted, and had never been more frightened in her life, but she still felt a sense of accomplishment. Even if she couldn't get him on the bed, she had him in the house.

Should she put him on the bed?

She looked at him lying on the kitchen floor. Still completely out cold. It worried her that he hadn't woken up the entire time. What was she going to do if he never woke up?

Fear cut through her again, sharp and hot and debilitating. She wanted to curl up in a ball on the floor. She had already done more than she ever thought she could. Just yesterday, she would have said she would have never been able to do that. And while she did feel a sense of accomplishment, it was really overshadowed by the fear.

She took a deep breath and tried to push it away. She could be afraid later. But for now, Asher needed her, and she couldn't not help him. She couldn't just sit around, not when there were things she could do. She had gotten him in the house, and that was a start. Now, she was going to find something to press against his temple to see if she could get that bleeding to stop.

He had a well pump handle in the sink, since there was no running water, and she hadn't tried to figure out how to work it that morning. She'd been able to cook the eggs and bacon without water. She figured he'd show her when he got back, but...now it was up to her.

She wracked her brain, trying to think if she'd ever seen a TV show that used one of these things. It seemed like she had, but she couldn't quite picture it in her mind. But the handle seemed like it would be something that she could just pull up, or maybe lift up and down?

She pulled it up, nothing happened, so she decided to move it up and down and see if that did something.

Nothing happened for the first few pumps, and she was about to give up, when a little trickle of water came out the spout.

It worked! She started pumping faster, and a big gush of water came out.

Awesome. She grinned, grabbing the roll of paper towels he had sitting on the counter. She hadn't used any so far, and wasn't sure what he did with his trash, so figured that he probably used them sparingly. But this seemed like a good use for one, so she wet it, wrung it out a little, and hurried back to where he lay on the floor.

On the spot, she decided she was going to keep him on the floor and would bring the blankets from the bed out and try to shift them underneath him.

Now that she wasn't working to drag a man across the yard, she realized it felt chilly in the cabin.

She needed to keep him warm. She was pretty sure on *Dr. MD*, which she hadn't watched in over a year, it had said something about people who were injured going into shock and keeping them warm. Or something like that.

She couldn't tell whether he was in shock or not... It had something to do with the heartbeat, she thought.

She really had no idea. She should pay more attention to that. Or she should watch documentaries on emergency first aid, and she would have, if she had known that at one point in her life, she was going to have to use that information.

Asher had been kind to her, he was going to take her home, and he only brought her because she said it was okay. She couldn't blame him for the predicament they were in.

Actually, it had been fun for a while. They'd had a good time in the grocery store, and...she had realized what a nice person he was.

She kind of liked him. Like, knew that he wasn't that little kid who was so much younger than she was that she didn't pay any attention to. But that he was...a man

This was a great time to figure that out. She wasn't even sure why she was thinking about that. She didn't know if he was going to make it. Why would she be thinking about how he was all grown up and she hadn't even noticed?

Rolling her eyes at how ridiculous a person could be, maybe it was the stress, she pressed the paper towel against his cut and held it there. Thinking. Making a mental list in her head.

She wasn't going to try to get him on the bed. It was higher than the steps, and she only brought him up the steps because she had to. She didn't want to manhandle him any more than what she had to.

So she'd bring the blankets out, put them by the stove, and then... She should make sure the fire didn't go out.

She had no idea how to handle a fire, but there was still wood in the box, so she would make him a bed, fix the fire, and pray. Maybe she should pray first, oh, and make sure that his head stopped bleeding.

There. That was her list of things to do. She could multitask and pray while she was doing the other three things. *Lord, please give me wisdom. I have no idea what to do. But You do. I'm sure You do. Just...help me. Please.*

She opened her eyes, and they drifted over to the windowsill where Asher's Bible still sat.

She'd made a promise to the Lord, and as soon as she had everything on her list done, she was going to keep it.

Chapter Eleven

An hour and a half later, Asher's temple still seeped blood, but she had cleaned the floor, laid blankets out, and rolled him on top of them. She'd added a couple of pieces of wood to the fire, prayed that it would continue to burn, and even ate some of the cold eggs on the table. Asher couldn't eat, hadn't woken up at all, but if she was going to care for him and get out of here herself, she needed to keep her strength up.

The thought she was trying not to think about was, if he didn't wake up, she was going to have to figure out how to get out on her own.

She considered walking for help, but if it was an hour drive to the last store, she would have to leave Asher for at least a day and maybe more. She was loath to do that.

It was late afternoon according to her calculations by the time she had everything situated, and she sat down beside him, with his Bible on her lap.

If he didn't wake up in the next hour, she was going to go looking for the keys to his pickup, and then, if she was able to find them, she would make a decision about whether or not she should go for help, since that meant leaving him alone. And driving a truck she wasn't sure she knew how to, and going on roads that she had no clue where they led. Including dirt roads. She could end up leaving him, getting lost, and both of them dying.

But if he...didn't make it, she was going to have to figure out how to get out of there on her own anyway.

The thoughts were starting to overwhelm her again, the fear crashing over her, and she tried to rein it in. She hated being afraid.

Taking his Bible, she tried to figure out where in the world she would start reading. She really didn't have a clue, so she opened it, aiming for the middle.

Psalms. She was familiar with some of them. The one about the Lord being her Shepherd or whatever. It didn't make a whole lot of sense to her, since she didn't know much about shepherds and sheep, and the imagery didn't make a lot of sense, but it sounded nice.

But as she looked down, it wasn't the shepherd Psalm that his Bible had opened to. It was Psalm 121, and she almost laughed as she read it:

I will lift up mine eyes unto the hills, from whence cometh my help. My help cometh from the Lord, which made heaven and earth.

How ironic. Here she was in the hills, and this was where God was supposed to be?

He will not suffer thy foot to be moved: he that keepeth thee will not slumber.

That was reassuring. God didn't sleep. And He wouldn't be moved. He was solid, someone she could depend on. She read that much of the Psalm again, then she read it again. Closing her eyes, she said it to herself.

God was here. God would not slumber. God would not be moved. God was in the hills, God made heaven and earth. I don't have to be afraid.

It's funny how just saying those things to herself didn't make her fear go away, but it made it less...strong. She could see how if she kept at it, maybe it would go away completely. She could depend totally on the Lord, and He would be there for her.

She sat there for a long time, just studying that one psalm. Not thinking about it any deeper than just believing what it said. God was here. He was her help. He made heaven and earth. He did not sleep.

He was her help.

Time flew by as she sat there thinking, and before she knew it, it was time to put another log on the fire.

Touching Asher, making sure that he didn't feel cold, she shifted.

And then she stopped, her eyes caught on his face. His eyes were closed, and a couple of times it was like he was in pain, with his brows furrowed, even while he slept.

But now they seemed more relaxed.

She hadn't really been reading much out loud, but...maybe that would be something that would help him.

As she shifted, the Bible closed, and she felt a little sad that she had lost her place, but she set it aside.

She ran her hand down his cheek; it didn't feel hot or feverish, but it didn't feel chilled either.

The stubble was rough against her fingers, and she paused again, thinking that the boy that she thought of when she thought of him was long gone. He was definitely all grown up. She hadn't really noticed.

She smiled when she thought of their banter in the grocery store, about how they had eight blocks of cream cheese in the refrigerator.

The eggs had been terrible, although cold eggs were never good. Maybe if she'd eaten them when they were hot, she would have a new favorite food.

"Maybe I'll just eat cream cheese for lunch. It's definitely after lunch. Although, I ate breakfast late, and I'm not very hungry." She looked over at him. His eyes were still closed. "Tell you what, when you wake up, we'll eat cream cheese together."

His eyelashes didn't flutter, and he didn't move at all. She opened her hand and ran her palm down his cheek. It was almost a caress, but it was more of a pleading from her for him to wake up.

"It's selfish, but I'm here by myself and I'm scared. I'd really like it if you'd wake up."

He didn't move. And she shifted, standing to her feet, reaching down, and setting the Bible on the table. She grabbed some wood, put it in the fire, and knew that there was probably something she should do with the stove, but she wasn't sure what. So she just closed the door, prayed it would keep burning, and then sniffed. Something stunk.

It took her a few minutes to realize it was the bedpan that she'd used that morning.

She had noticed it a little when she grabbed the blankets to make a bed for Asher. She had to go in and check the drawers, and she found some extra blankets, although there was only one pillow, and so she took it from the bed and used it for him. She figured he needed it more than she did, especially considering that the floor was probably hard.

But at the time, she'd been so busy trying to get things settled she hadn't thought about the smell. Now, it really bothered her.

Well, she had to go out sometime, and who knew how long she was going to be here with Asher. Even if he did wake up, which... She really hoped he would wake up. Even though she doubted he would be up to driving for a while. After the blow he'd taken to his head, it would probably be safer if he didn't.

So, she was going to have to learn to use the outhouse, and she would rather do it during the daylight. Grabbing the bedpan and holding it as far away from her body as she could, she stepped around Asher and walked outside.

Dumping it out was one thing, but then she realized she probably should rinse it out. She didn't really want to take it to the sink in the kitchen, so...she listened, looking around and walking the short distance to the creek.

It was kind of pretty, with some big rocks with green moss on them and the sparkling water gurgling and bubbling as it happily found its way around them.

It did seem happy, the creek. Which was weird, since she knew creeks didn't have emotions.

Still, she never really thought of a creek in any way before and smiled at the idea that it was a cheerful little thing, over here beside the cabin.

She rinsed the bedpan out and then walked back, stopping at the outhouse.

It wasn't an emergency that she went, but she did have to go. And... She took in a deep breath and blew it out. She could do this.

Opening the door, checking for critters, she put one foot inside and then the other. Asher was not there to check it for her, nor was he there to stand outside in case she needed help, and she definitely missed him.

But nothing happened. She was completely safe, and other than an odd noise, which she wasn't sure what it was, she managed to put her bare bottom over that dark, scary hole and do what she needed to do.

It was a relief when she walked out the door.

She hated the outhouse. Hated it.

As she bent to pick up the bedpan, she realized that she didn't have to use the outhouse. She could go to the bathroom in the woods if she felt like it. There was no one there to see.

Although it would probably be wise to dig a hole. But...keeping everything in one spot seemed somehow more civilized.

Or of course she could continue to go in the bedpan, but realizing now that someone had to empty the bedpan, or it would cause the entire house to stink, she decided that...maybe she'd just keep using the outhouse.

Hopefully it wouldn't be long, though. Hopefully when she walked in the house, Asher would be up, and he would be fine.

Somehow she thought that was maybe wishful thinking, but she supposed wishful thinking was better than fearful thinking.

The sun was still up in the beautiful blue sky, the puffy white clouds were still there, and suddenly she realized it could be raining. It could be dark. It could be cold. And yet, she had stopped to appreciate the fact that at least if she had to have something like this happen to her, it happened on a really nice day.

That seemed like a silly thing to thank God for, but she stopped right there in the path and bowed her head.

Lord, thank you so much for the beautiful day. I'm scared, I don't know what I'm going to do, and I'm paranoid that Asher is going to be permanently hurt, either because of me or because of the tree. Either way, I don't want him to be. I don't want anything to happen to him.

She tried to pull her thoughts back to the gratefulness that she had been feeling earlier. Not to fall into the pit of fear and anxiety. *I just wanted to thank You for the nice day. The good weather. It's a great day to pull a guy out of the woods, so, yeah. Thanks.*

She laughed to herself. Obviously, she needed some work on her prayers. It was a great day to pull a guy out of the woods? Man. God must be shaking His head at her right now. Although, maybe God was just happy to hear from her.

There was a part of her that wished that she had her phone, because this would make for some great viral videos, but she realized that she hadn't thought about her TV shows in a long time. Other than trying to figure out if she learned anything that would be helpful to her situation.

She hadn't really missed them. She hadn't died, anyway.

Stepping up on the porch, she walked in, holding her breath and hoping that Asher was awake. But his eyes were closed, and he lay exactly as she left him. She couldn't help that her heart sank clear to her toes, and fear started to take over again.

Her eyes landed on the Bible that still lay on the table.

Maybe it was time for a little more reading. This time, she'd read out loud. After all, maybe Asher could hear, and surely that would be a comfort to him, hearing God's word.

She liked the Psalms, and so, she settled herself down beside Asher, putting a hand on his forehead to make sure that he wasn't too hot. It wasn't feverish and wasn't cold. Then she ran her palm down his cheek like she had before. His stubble had grown a bit, and if he were awake, she might tell him that she liked it.

She shook her head. No. Of course she would not do that.

Taking the Bible, she allowed it to fall open at the middle again. This time, her eyes caught on Psalm 91. And she started reading it aloud.

He that dwelleth in the secret place of the most High shall abide under the shadow of the Almighty.

I will say of the LORD, He is my refuge and my fortress: my God; in him will I trust.

Surely he shall deliver thee from the snare of the fowler, and from the noisome pestilence.

He shall cover thee with his feathers, and under his wings shalt thou trust: his truth shall be thy shield and buckler.

Thou shalt not be afraid for the terror by night; nor for the arrow that flieth by day;

Nor for the pestilence that walketh in darkness; nor for the destruction that wasteth at noonday.

A thousand shall fall at thy side, and ten thousand at thy right hand; but it shall not come nigh thee.

Only with thine eyes shalt thou behold and see the reward of the wicked.

Because thou hast made the LORD, which is my refuge, even the most High, thy habitation;

There shall no evil befall thee, neither shall any plague come nigh thy dwelling.

For he shall give his angels charge over thee, to keep thee in all thy ways.

They shall bear thee up in their hands, lest thou dash thy foot against a stone.

Thou shalt tread upon the lion and adder: the young lion and the dragon shalt thou trample under feet.

Because he hath set his love upon me, therefore will I deliver him: I will set him on high, because he hath known my name.

He shall call upon me, and I will answer him: I will be with him in trouble; I will deliver him, and honour him.

With long life will I satisfy him, and shew him my salvation.

She got to the end, and her eye caught on that last verse. With long life. She glanced down at Asher. She hoped he had a long life. Longer than the thirty-some years that he'd already lived.

She looked back down at her Bible. It said:

Because he has set his love upon me, therefore will I deliver him.

She supposed that meant that having a long life was contingent on loving God. Being delivered was contingent on loving God.

That made her think. She hadn't been very good at loving God. She considered herself a Christian and would have said that she did love God, but...how had she shown it? By putting Him dead last in her life?

After her shows. After her movies. After all the trivia that she knew about every actor and actress who'd ever played on anything that she enjoyed and a lot of things she hadn't.

God might be at the end of that list.

She hadn't given Him much time at all. In fact, as she thought about it, she could definitely quote more lines of movies, TV shows, and was more familiar with those kinds of things than she was with the Bible in general. Or with the Bible in particular. She didn't think she had a single verse memorized. Maybe she knew John 3:16.

But random lines of movies popped out at her, and she knew them all. She could even say what actor had said them. And quote them word for word.

That was sad.

Well. She hadn't realized until just now how sad that was. Sad that she'd call herself a Christian, yet she knew more about Hollywood than she did about God. She'd definitely spent more time with Hollywood.

Well, she wanted a long life, she wanted God to protect her. And she wanted Him to know that she loved Him. To her, love meant spending time with someone. Love meant knowing them. Knowing their likes and dislikes, and talking to them too.

She put her head down and read the entire Psalm again. Instead of the Hollywood junk that was in her brain, the junk which didn't help her or keep her from being scared, the best thing that she could do would be to put this psalm in her brain, hide it in her heart. Memorize it.

So, for the next...she didn't know how long because she didn't have any way to keep track of time, she worked on memorizing that chapter. She did it out loud, just because she didn't know whether hearing her voice, hearing God's word, would help Asher or not.

By the time she was ready to quit, dusk had started to fall, and a curl of fear started in her stomach. She didn't want to spend the night alone. Of course, Asher was there, but he was hardly with her if he was unconscious, right?

Still, she probably should eat something, so she got the leftover bacon out of the refrigerator where she set it, and...her eyes landed on the cream cheese. All seven and a half packages. Smiling a little, she got one package.

Yeah. She'd have cream cheese and bacon for supper.

And she wasn't going to eat at the table. She'd sit down beside Asher. Just in case he was able to understand things, she was going to explain that she was going to try to make sure that his cream cheese didn't go to waste. And she was more than willing to share.

Turned out, she didn't have to share anything, because Asher didn't wake up. Not while she was eating, not after she finished. Not while she figured out how to do the dishes with cold water and one paper towel.

She put another log on the fire, and although she was dreading it, she knew she needed to walk out to the outhouse at least one more time.

She didn't want to, for sure she didn't want to, but...she needed to unless she wanted to use the bedpan.

She thought about the flashlight and decided she would take that. She knew he had said it was for emergencies, and she didn't want to waste the battery or anything. But goodness knew she'd had more emergencies today than she had expected in her life, ever, so she pampered herself a little and decided she'd feel better with the light. Even though it wasn't completely dark.

"I'll be right back. I'm going to use the outhouse. I...hate using the outhouse, but I hate even worse emptying the bedpan and having to wash it out. I did it in the creek, by the way, just so you know I didn't do that in the sink." She laughed a little, even though Asher's face did not move at all.

She put a hand on his cheek, palm down, feeling the prickly stubble and...the square jaw and thinking about the night before, when he tried to talk to her about how much he loved the stars and sitting out at night and listening to the sounds, and how...how that had scared her. She hadn't wanted to talk about it. She wanted to go inside where it was nice and bright and the light chased away all the shadows. She didn't want to enjoy the night.

She swallowed hard.

"Sorry about last night. You... You obviously love it here, and...I was kinda self-centered, actually, I was a lot self-centered. I'm sorry. I don't think I'm going to try to enjoy the night right now, but if you wake up,

I'll sit with you and maybe listen, look, and smell." She laughed a little. "But first, I'm going to go out there to that outhouse, and I'm going to use it." She nodded her head and stood to her feet.

She walked into the bedroom to grab the flashlight and walked back out.

Asher hadn't moved.

She sighed. She'd only been doing this for less than a day, and already she was struggling to keep a brave front. She wanted to cry. She'd wanted to cry all day, but hadn't.

Maybe she could light the lamp and read the Bible a little more when she came back. The thought made the fear not quite so bad, and she walked out, heading toward the outhouse, slowly, watching for any animals that might be around.

The clearing was still light, but as she hit the path for the outhouse, it started to get darker.

Peering into the woods, it was dark all around.

That was something she hadn't thought about before. It would get dark sooner in the woods than it would in the clearing. Of course.

Maybe that was information she'd need in the future, maybe not, but it was definitely something she hadn't thought about before.

Regardless, she made it to the outhouse and opened the door boldly.

There was a flash of movement, a hiss and a screech, and she screamed, dropping the flashlight in her haste to get away. She scrambled back, tripping over a root? Air? She wasn't sure, but she ended up landing hard on her butt, looking at an animal that had climbed halfway up the doorway of the outhouse. A raccoon?

She had never been that close to a wild animal before, a wild animal of any kind, but she was pretty sure that was a raccoon.

It was gray and had stripes, and that black mask over its eyes that... she was pretty sure meant it was a raccoon.

It didn't look cute and cuddly, it looked ferocious and scary, and then as she watched, a little nose poked around the side of the outhouse, sniffing, before it moseyed into the open doorway. A baby? Despite the fact that her heart seemed to be jumping out of her chest and she was terrified, the baby was absolutely adorable.

She wanted to get away, but she was afraid to move, to draw attention to herself and have the mama raccoon attack her, but her attention was drawn to the baby and how cute it was.

Then, another one showed up behind the first one. And then, as she watched, one, two, three more. Five babies gathered around the entrance to the door and then started climbing up the side of the opening, after their mom.

Their mom, moving her head around, sniffing the air, hadn't moved from her position.

Sondra wasn't sure if they could see very well, but surely she could smell.

The claws that the mom used to grip the side looked sharp and long and very, very wicked.

Sondra considered scooting the whole way back to the cabin on her butt, keeping her eye on the raccoon, but she hadn't made any move toward her and seemed more concerned about getting her family organized as she looked behind her and chirped. It wasn't exactly a chirp. Maybe a churr.

At any rate, the mama raccoon started backing down, and the babies backed down out of her way.

The sound that she made seemed familiar, and Sondra remembered the noise she'd heard earlier when she'd been in the outhouse. Had that been the raccoon talking to her babies? Did they have some kind of nest inside the outhouse? Was it...in the hole?

No... Surely not. She didn't look like she had any kind of dirt on her, and none of the babies did either. They looked remarkably clean.

The mama managed to get back down and stood in the doorway, looking directly at Sondra and sniffing.

Sondra held her breath and didn't move a muscle.

A thought flashed through her brain. She wished she had her phone, that it was charged, that she could take a video. This was a video worth posting.

But she didn't, and she was afraid to move anyway.

The mom must have decided that everything was okay, because she stepped down off the outhouse floor and led the little parade around the outhouse and into the woods down toward the creek.

Sondra sat on the ground, her heart beating hard, and while her mind told her that the danger, such as it was, had passed, the rest of her was taking a little bit longer to respond. Her lungs still felt like she needed to gasp for air, and her body didn't want to move.

She realized that her butt hurt. Between landing on it so hard and the briar that had been stuck in it earlier, it had taken a beating today.

This seemed like a good time to curl into a ball and cry. But maybe she ought to wait until she got back to the cabin for that.

Looking around for the flashlight, she stuck her head into the opening of the outhouse, turning the beam on and shining it around.

Sure enough, there was a spot by the rafters that looked like it would be big enough for a raccoon and her babies. It wasn't huge, but she supposed that raccoons didn't need a living room and a dining room and bedroom and bathroom, the way a human might. So, it was probably big enough.

She sighed. What a day. It wasn't even over, Asher hadn't woken up, and tomorrow she might have to think a little harder on what she was going to do if Asher *didn't* wake up.

That was something she didn't want to think about, had been pushing aside for most of the day, but it was probably something she was going to have to face.

She had never looked for the keys to the pickup, other than a cursory search around the cabin.

So on the way back from the outhouse, she stopped at his pickup, opening the door and looking. She remembered specifically seeing him taking the keys out of the ignition and putting them in his pocket.

She hadn't checked his pocket.

So, after looking around in all the obvious spots, she closed the pickup door and walked to the cabin. She didn't take very long, since it seemed like every second it got darker, and she did not want to be out in the woods in the dark.

Walking into the cabin, closing the door behind her, she leaned back with a sigh of relief. She wouldn't have to open it until tomorrow, but... She looked at the woodbox. It was almost empty. Tomorrow might end up being harder than today.

She took one step before her eyes dropped to Asher, and she realized he was looking at her.

85

Chapter Twelve

Asher blinked and looked around.

Trying to remember, although it was hard to think with the pounding in his head. Pain seemed to radiate up and down his body, maybe focusing especially on his ribs. Particularly on his left side.

He hurt. Everything hurt.

Even opening his eyes seemed to hurt.

But...he thought he remembered... Did Sondra offer him water last night? And cream cheese. She offered him cream cheese.

No. That couldn't possibly be right. Why would she do that? What a weird dream.

But why did he hurt so much? And where was he? And why was Sondra in his dreams?

Actually, Sondra spent a lot of time in his dreams, so that wasn't a huge question, but it felt so odd.

Actually, everything felt odd. Like he was lying on...the floor. He moved his hand, stifling a groan, because even that small movement hurt. But yeah. It felt hard underneath him, but was he at the cabin?

There was a soft hand on his face. It touched over his nose, across his cheek, and he blinked, trying to clear his eyes, squinting, trying to look through the fog of pain and confusion.

Sondra.

She had two heads. So it had to be a dream. Because in real life, Sondra only had one head. He was pretty sure about that.

One head, one body. And one great big personality.

He almost smiled, but he had a feeling that that would hurt too. "Asher?"

Now two-headed Sondra was talking to him. Odd. It even had Sondra's voice.

It seemed like both mouths were moving.

"You have two heads."

That seemed like an obvious statement, but he just wanted whatever it was to know that he was on to it. It wasn't fooling him. Sondra hadn't suddenly come and started taking care of him. Wherever he was.

Maybe it was heaven. Did people have two heads in heaven? He'd never read that in the Bible. He figured they'd have long white robes. If that was God's dress standard, he wondered if maybe he should wear robes now. A long white one. But people already thought his family was weird. If he started walking around in a long white robe, they might take him away.

"Can you hear me, Asher?"

He tried to bring his mind back. Back to...he wasn't sure. Was this reality? Where someone or something, the look-alike Sondra, but with two heads, and a very, very soft touch, and Sondra's voice, was leaning over him, asking if he was okay.

"I know who you are." He tried to sound threatening, but to his ears, he just sounded weak.

She laughed a little. "Oh really? Say my name then."

The heads were kind of wavering back and forth. Maybe there was a third head in there. Maybe he had miscounted. Surely he could count to three. He'd done it all his life. Most of it. Had he suddenly forgotten how to count?

He squinted, and all three heads merged into one. One beautiful, beautiful head.

And then they diverged again.

Odd. Fake Sondra was acting really oddly. Like it wasn't quite real. Maybe it was some kind of artificial intelligence. He heard that artificial intelligence was getting even more intelligent, which, in Asher's opinion, it wasn't going to take much intelligence to overtake the human race. Men seemed to be getting dumber rather than smarter.

But that was negative thinking.

He wasn't supposed to do negative thinking, although...he couldn't really think of anything positive right now. Everything hurt, he seemed to be lying on the floor somewhere, and someone with two heads who was pretending to be Sondra was leaning over top of him asking if he was okay. Then demanding that he say its name.

"You look like Sondra," he mumbled. His voice was not nearly as strong as he wanted it to be. "But I know you're not. You're not fooling me."

"Oh, I'm not?" the thing said, leaning even closer. "Asher. You scared me to death. Are you thirsty?"

He scared her/it? That was interesting. It didn't seem to be going to hurt him. And he was thirsty. So thirsty he could barely stand it, but...he also had to go to the bathroom.

He wasn't quite sure how he was going to tell fake Sondra that he needed her to leave.

He had to get to the bathroom.

"Yes," he croaked, hoping that getting a drink would distract her, and he could jump up and go to the bathroom, except as she turned, and he tried to move, he realized he wasn't going to jump anywhere. Sharp pain crashed up and down his rib cage, turning his entire world red and black. He realized the sound he heard was himself groaning.

"Asher! Don't move!"

It was going to be very difficult to go to the bathroom without moving.

And he wasn't going to be able to wait much longer.

"Drink," he managed to mutter. And she left him again.

He thought she gave him a dark look, threatening him, like she was warning him that he better not get up and go anywhere without her, but she didn't understand. He needed to.

He closed his eyes, thinking that he needed to rest for a minute, but then fake Sondra was back before he had another opportunity to try to use the restroom.

"I'm going to put my hand under your head and lift it up. I didn't fill the glass very full, so we won't spill it all over you. Okay?"

He started to nod but couldn't because her hand was already under his head, so he just grunted.

"Does it hurt?"

Everything hurt. He wasn't quite sure what exactly she was asking him about at this time, but he said, "Drink."

She didn't say anything more, just lifted his head up, and he needed a moment to let the excruciating pain die down. She put the glass to his lips, and he hoped she didn't drown him before he was able to open his mouth and swallow. He just needed a minute. Needed to let the sharp throbbing turn into something he could stand before he could open his mouth and think about swallowing.

"Asher. You have to open your mouth."

Uh. He knew it. He knew it.

Breathing hurt. He couldn't even take a deep breath; trying to fill his lungs up more than just a little bit was too hard.

He opened his mouth; surely he could swallow a little.

Thankfully, she didn't dump the whole thing in, so she must not mean to kill him right away. Because she could have drowned him pretty easily. Come to think of it, she could have taken the knife out of the drawer and slit his throat with it. So, maybe fake Sondra wasn't trying to kill him after all. Or maybe she wanted him in a little better condition before she decided to off him.

Whatever it was, the first swallow of water slid down his throat with quenching relief, and he took as much water as she would give him.

It might have been only a quarter of a glass, but it tasted so sweet and so good, and he wanted to just sit and drink and drink all day long.

But he still had that problem.

"Leave," he said, realizing that things were becoming a little clearer. He was pretty sure he was in his cabin. Pretty sure he remembered... Did he bring Sondra to his cabin? Why would he have done this?

His head hurt, and he couldn't quite put the picture of the day before or whenever it was together. Couldn't quite fit the pieces of how he had gotten to be lying on the floor in a massive amount of pain so they made a rational memory.

Just bits and pieces jumped into his head here and there.

He didn't have amnesia. Because he knew his name. It was...Asher. Asher and this woman, who looked like Sondra and now mostly only had one head. Maybe he had double vision because... Had he gotten hit on the head somehow? It sure did hurt.

He moved two fingers up to try to touch it and see.

"Don't touch that. It's still kind of wet and probably should have been stitched, but I couldn't find any bandages, and I definitely was not putting any stitches in your head."

Yeah. That sounded like Sondra. Except... How had he gotten a gash in his head?

"Leave," he muttered. Wondering why she didn't just listen to him. He tried to say it forcefully, but even to himself, it sounded weak and pathetic.

"I am staying right here beside you. I am not leaving you. Now, if you'd like some more water, I will see to that. And... Actually, I might have to leave you. There's no more wood for the fire."

His eyes shifted to the stove. It wasn't very far from him. He was on the floor beside it. Why wasn't he in bed? If he was so sore and whatever was wrong with him, shouldn't he be in bed?

"Leave." He said it as loud as he could, as forcefully, as commanding as he could. She needed to go.

"I am not leaving."

He opened his eyes, trying to glare at her, she glared right back down at him, and even though she was sitting beside him, her hands were on her hips or thighs or something.

He narrowed his eyes. Were those scratches on her face? What happened? Did he wreck his pickup?

"I need..." What did he need? Something.

"What? Tell me. I'll get you whatever you need. Well, if I have it."

"I need..."

"Asher. Tell me!"

"Pee. I need to pee."

He wasn't so out of it that he hadn't figured out something had happened. Some kind of accident, something where he had gotten hurt. It looked like she did too. But she was up and moving around, so...

maybe he protected her. That was a nice thought. And maybe it really was Sondra. He thought it was.

She gasped. "Oh! I hadn't thought of that. Of course. Um... I'm not sure how that's going to happen."

If he wasn't in so much pain, he would smile. Laugh at her obvious distress. For him, it wasn't exactly something he wanted to do in front of her, but the feeling that if they ended up having to do it together, she was going to be the one who was more embarrassed, made him want to smile all the same.

He was going to have to be unconscious for them to do it together though. He didn't want to embarrass her. And it didn't feel very manly to not be able to use the restroom by himself. Except, since he couldn't even get up off the ground, it was a distinct possibility that he was going to need help.

"Well, we have the bedpan." Her voice kind of trailed off, like she wasn't sure exactly what they were going to do with the bedpan. "How much of this do you think you can do by yourself?"

Her voice sounded a little panicked.

He really wanted to laugh.

"No! You are not allowed to smile over this. You wipe that off your face this second, young man," she said, and she pointed at his lips.

"If it didn't hurt so much, I'd laugh."

"This is not funny. This is not the slightest bit funny."

"It kind of is."

He might be going to die. He really didn't know. If the pain in his body was any indication, he really thought he was going to, but did the fact that he was going to die make it necessary for him to be serious? He didn't think so. Maybe he didn't quite have all of his reasoning facilities back, but he was pretty sure that if he was going to die, he wanted to die laughing.

"You know what would be funny? If I would leave you. That would be hilarious. Although, I do have to warn you, you have a family of raccoons living in your outhouse."

"Stop it. I can't laugh. It hurts."

His brain fog cleared enough that he was pretty sure that he figured out what was going on. He brought Sondra up to get her away from Ezra, because Ezra was getting married to someone else.

He had a crush on Sondra. That wasn't something he had to figure out. It had been a part of him for so long that it was just accepted. And he'd gone out to cut firewood. Yesterday? Sunday. Whatever day it was. And the last thing he remembered was hearing a big crack and looking up. Maybe something had fallen on him? A branch? That made sense.

Or it might have fallen down. But he didn't think he cut himself with his chainsaw. It would be kinda hard, although that might explain the gash on his temple, but it didn't explain the pain throughout the rest of his body.

"Here. I'll set the bedpan right here, and... I... I guess I could unbuckle your pants for you. But you're going to have to do the rest. Do you think you can do that?"

He wanted to say he could. But he wasn't sure. He did appreciate her offering to unbuckle his pants, as much as he didn't want to admit it. Just trying to use his arm with that kind of pressure he knew would be extremely painful.

"I'll try." His voice sounded a little bit firmer than it had, but the pain was almost unbearable.

He closed his eyes while she set the bedpan down. He heard a click on the floor. And then clothing rustled as she moved over him.

Chapter Thirteen

I t was ironic, the fact that Asher had a crush on Sondra forever, and here she was, unbuttoning his pants. And he was embarrassed. Rather than...excited? This wasn't exactly how he ever thought this would go. Although, it was a little bit of a fantasy for him.

Still, he kept his lips tightly shut around that. In his weakened state, he didn't want to accidentally tell her anything that might alert her to the fact that he had unremitted feelings for her.

"There. Do you think you can take it from here? I hate to leave you high and dry, but...I guess I've already done a bunch of things that I didn't think I could do. I suppose I could do this too." She sounded uncertain.

"I think I can," he said, not opening his eyes. He would have to. He would make himself do it. "What happened?" Maybe that would help him figure out what he could use and what he couldn't.

"I'm not sure. You went out to get wood. And when you didn't come back, I... I went out after you. I wasn't sure what happened, and I was kind of scared."

He bet she was scared. He could only imagine. She hated the mountains, and he shouldn't have brought her here.

"I wasn't sure whether maybe a serial killer had gotten you. Or something."

"Not a serial killer." His lips curved up again. Goodness, she had an active imagination. Wouldn't a serial killer who wanted to kill people go somewhere where there actually were people? Not in the middle of the mountains, where there wasn't another soul for miles.

"Anyway, maybe a wild animal. Are there bears around here? Cougars? I don't know, elephants or tigers or lions or cheetahs or something."

That time, he did laugh, but he regretted it, because it hurt, a lot. He groaned.

"Stop it. I hate it when you're hurting."

"Me too." He opened one eye and gave her an ironic look.

It was a look that made her laugh, as he had intended, and that made him smile. "That right there makes me feel better than anything," he said.

"What?" she asked, looking around, puzzled.

"You laughing."

He closed his eyes. There. He said something that he didn't want to. He needed to shut up. Otherwise, he was going to be spilling everything to her, and that would be no good. He'd be embarrassed as soon as he was able to get up and get around, and she would demand he take her home, and then she'd never speak to him again.

When he had thought that taking her to his mountain cabin for a week would give him a chance to let her get to know him and possibly for them to develop a relationship, this was not what he had in mind.

Her helping him use the restroom was way further along in a relationship than what he wanted to be.

He wasn't even sure he wanted to be that far along with his wife.

"All right. I don't know how to get you to let me know if you need help. I guess just yell? I'll stand on the other side of the kitchen with my back to you?"

A memory, fuzzy at first, flashed through his head. Her demanding that he hold his fingers in his ears while he stood outside the outhouse so she could go and he wouldn't listen to her apparently.

He allowed his lips to curve up. "Only if you put your fingers in your ears."

She stared at him for just a second before her face lit up and her laughter rang out again. "You're not as bad off as what you act like, if you remember all that."

"Kinda hard to forget."

"Fine. I'll put my fingers in my ears," she said, rolling her eyes as she stood to her feet.

He shook his head and then immediately regretted it as pain coursed through him.

"I was kidding," he mumbled, his voice much more subdued as he waited for the pain to subside. Man, he didn't know it was possible for a person to hurt this much. But from what she said, he got hit by a branch, not run over by a truck or anything, so...he doubted he had any internal injuries. Just a really bad concussion, and maybe some broken ribs.

He wasn't quite sure how all that could have happened, but it seemed trees sometimes did some pretty wild things when he'd been cutting them down. Including one that had fallen down, hit something, and jumped backward. Thankfully, it had fallen to the other side of the stump from where he stood, but if he had been cutting from the other side, the tree would have hit him and at the very least knocked him out. It could have ended up falling on him.

But those were the kind of freak accidents that a person couldn't prevent. He was always careful when he was cutting trees down, and he did what he could to minimize the risk of an accident, but ultimately, God was in control.

He had no idea what the Lord was doing, allowing this to happen, but... He grinned a little. Maybe God was being a matchmaker. After all, Sondra had wanted to go home, and he had been going to take her after she got up. But he couldn't, since he'd been knocked out.

Well, whoever said the Lord works in mysterious ways certainly knew what they were talking about. Maybe the Almighty really was a matchmaker. Although, he wasn't sure whether he should be grateful about that or not. He was in an awful lot of pain.

But he supposed he shouldn't look a gift horse in the mouth, and if this was the way that the Lord had for him to spend more time with Sondra, he supposed he should just suck it up.

And he needed to start working on the bathroom thing. It was just in the nick of time, since he didn't think he could hold it for another second.

It was painful, slow, arduous, and he was panting once he was done. He also thought he might not have quite gotten everything into the pan.

Which was extremely embarrassing.

That was more embarrassing than having Sondra help him. For him anyway. He thought she would be far less embarrassed to know that he hadn't quite been able to accomplish what he set out to do than for her to have had to help him.

He set the pan aside. That was kind of embarrassing too. She was going to have to deal with it.

Pain radiated up and down his spine, hot and fiery, and he was exhausted from just that little bit.

"Are you done?" she asked from the other side of the room.

"Almost," he said wearily. He hadn't gotten himself covered back up. He needed to regroup and get some strength back first.

"What are you doing?" she asked, and maybe he should have been irritated that she didn't seem to be able to give a man who had just been knocked out by a tree more than a few minutes to go to the bathroom by himself, but it made him smile instead. Her impatience, her inability to stay quiet and still. She was probably dying without her phone.

Maybe he should tell her where his was. But... He hadn't even thought about his phone. It didn't really matter since there was no service at the cabin. He'd have to travel down the mountain almost to town to get a signal.

Gingerly, he moved his arm and adjusted things so that he was decent.

"I'm done," he said wearily. Some pain meds would be really nice right now. Actually, he thought he had some in the cupboard in a small box. It didn't look like a first-aid box, but he put some supplies in it to keep there. Nothing that would help if there was some kind of traumatic event, but bandages and gauze and painkillers.

"Oh my goodness. What did you do, take a nap?"

"Yeah. I had to rest halfway through."

"I'm sorry. I'm just...a little worried. Relieved, concerned, and deathly afraid."

"Afraid?"

"We're alone in the woods. I mean, I'm not used to not being around people. This is...scary."

"Only if you let it be. It could be the best experience of your life."

Maybe that was a bit of an exaggeration. But the idea that she might fall in love with him and consider this one of the best things that ever happened to her was something that his positive-thinking brain could not allow to go unthought. He wanted to take that thought and hold it close.

But he had to say, "I think I might have not quite gotten everything in the bedpan."

"Oh."

He couldn't tell whether it was disgust or surprise or just a casual "well, I'll take care of it" kind of "oh."

"I can take the blankets off the bed, make you a new pallet, and do you think you could roll over onto it?"

"How did you get me from outside into here? Did I get up and walk?" He could hardly believe it. The idea of sitting up made his brain spin.

"I dragged you."

"You?" He narrowed his eyes and looked at her. She was about half his size. She couldn't possibly have dragged him.

"The thirty extra pounds I have around the middle came in handy." She patted her stomach.

"I like it," he said simply.

She rolled her eyes but didn't argue.

Then he thought of something else. "How did you get me up the steps?"

"Well, I got behind you, lifted you up a bit, sat on the step, and kind of had you sitting between my legs, and I scooted up and dragged you up with me. I'm pretty sure it hurt you pretty bad."

"Yeah. That sounds really painful right now." He couldn't help wincing.

"I'm sure it was. You groaned several times, but never woke up."

He couldn't imagine her doing all that. But what else was she going to do? He was impressed that she had gotten him into the house. And he couldn't think of anything else she could have done better, unless she had known that he had a phone.

Of course, he kept his phone in the console of his pickup in the compartment there, because there was no service in the cabin. So there was no point in having it out.

He certainly was in no condition to drive an hour down the road in order to get service.

"Thanks. I appreciate you taking care of me." He couldn't believe that she had. "That must have taken a lot of courage."

"Yeah. It did. I still feel very afraid, but I hope you don't mind, I started reading your Bible."

"No. Go right ahead." He knew that made him smile, but he couldn't hide it.

"You don't have to laugh at me."

"I wasn't. I was just thinking, there's nothing like fear to drive us to the Lord. It's happened to me, over and over again."

"Really?"

"Sure. I mean, I guess we didn't really talk about it, but when I first came up here, I wasn't entirely comfortable being alone."

"You weren't?" She huffed out a laugh and shook her head. "I wouldn't have guessed that. You didn't say, and I thought there was something wrong with me because it scared me to death to be here by myself. Especially if...you never woke up."

He nodded, and the movement made his chest hurt, so he closed his eyes.

"You rest. We talked enough. Just ignore me if I start talking again, because I do have a tendency to talk to myself, it makes me feel a little less alone."

"Just don't argue with yourself. That would be weird."

"Actually, I have had several arguments with myself, just today, sorry."

"Who won?" He was mostly joking.

"I did, of course." She sounded a little flirty, and he really wanted to open his eyes to see her, see her smile, see her eyes sparkle, see that she was really there. And only had one head. That was kind of important too.

But he didn't, he kept his eyes closed and drifted in and out of sleep as she made another pallet and the bedpan disappeared.

She disappeared for a while too, and he assumed she was taking it and throwing it out, and rinsing the pan out. She must have found the creek. He hadn't thought to ask about it. He thought it was really pretty, and it was one of his favorite spots. When he was at the cabin, he was typically working, but when he took a break, and sometimes when he ate lunch and supper, he'd take it down to the creek and enjoy it there.

It was definitely a nice spot, and he really wanted to share it with her.

There was so much he wanted to share with her. Maybe he'd get a chance to, but he needed to remember that none of this might be for her. She hadn't said she all of a sudden decided to become a mountain girl. And he couldn't blame her if she didn't. He hadn't been joking that there were times where he'd wanted to get in his pickup and leave, just because it was too much to be so alone for so long, then he kind of got used to it and had come to enjoy it.

By the time she had the pallet made and asked him if he could move from one to the other, most of him had quit hurting. And he was loath to make himself start again. But he could smell the blankets, and they definitely needed to be washed. He supposed the sooner that happened, the better, although he felt bad about making more work for her.

She hadn't complained, and he actually heard her singing. She had a sweet voice, and it definitely soothed him. He hadn't asked her to start again after she quit, but maybe he would later. After he took a nap. He probably ought to figure out if there was anything wrong with him that would send him to the ER.

Later.

Chapter Fourteen

S ondra tapped the pencil against her temple as she looked at the verse she had just copied into her notebook.

This poor man cried, and the Lord heard him, and saved him out of all his troubles.

It had been two days since Asher had been knocked unconscious. Once he'd woken up, he had told her where his notebook and pencil were when she asked, and she'd also been able to move him to the bed.

The effort had almost made him pass out, and he had actually thrown up from the pain, which had made things even worse. He'd been in agony, and she felt so helpless and frustrated, because there wasn't anything she could do to help him, other than watch him suffer. She had even dragged his pallet over to the side of the bed, so all he had to do was lie back down.

She had thought he might be going to pass out several times. So she kind of felt like having him puke was the lesser of the two evils. For her anyway, even though it meant she had a mess to clean up. At least she didn't have an unconscious man on the floor again in some kind of heap.

If she had to do it over again, she would have been very firm in her refusal to allow him to move anywhere.

He had insisted that he would be able to get up to use the restroom. That was not happening. Not for a long, long time.

So far, in the two days that he'd been down, he'd eaten an entire block of cream cheese and half of another one.

She didn't feel the slightest bit bad giving it to him, either. She figured the calories were good for him, since that was all he had other than water. And at least if he threw up, there was no chance of him choking.

The fear that always was with her, the one she used the TV and her shows to keep at bay, had settled like a prickly ball of briars in her stomach.

She looked back down at what she had been writing, reading over the verses, saying them aloud.

But I am poor and needy; yet the Lord thinketh upon me: thou art my help and my deliverer; make no tarrying, O my God.

Help me, O LORD my God: O save me according to thy mercy:

Thou art near, O LORD; and all thy commandments are truth.

There were a whole lot more. And they had helped her. She had plenty of time to work on it. All Asher had seemed to do was sleep. He didn't even eat that much, other than the cream cheese, which seemed to be enough. Any movement seemed to hurt, although she thought his head felt better. She was pretty sure his ribs still pained him a lot. But together, they had figured out that they didn't think he had any internal injuries. He insisted that he didn't want to go anywhere but would rather recover at his cabin.

She had argued with him a bit, but mostly because of her own fear and not for his welfare, so she had quit as soon as she realized she wasn't really trying to do what was best for him.

His argument that he would heal better and faster if he was not in the hospital, surrounded by beeping machines and people who didn't know him, but rather stayed here, in the mountains, one of his favorite places in the world, breathing in the fresh air and relaxing in his own place, had been compelling.

She didn't think this would be the best place for her, but it wasn't about her.

Thankfully she figured that out before she insisted on her way.

Actually, she was kind of glad Asher had insisted, because...she could hardly believe she was thinking it, but she'd started to like it here. In the last few days, she kind of got into a routine, and the extra time to go through the Bible had been enlightening.

Asher had helped her a little bit, asking her what she knew, and some of the verses she was trying to memorize he already had put to memory and could listen and correct her when she got stuck.

He seemed to have an endless amount of patience, which was nice. It was opposite from her, since she had barely any. Patience was something she wanted more of, but in order to get patience, a person had to have their patience tested, and she didn't really like that. No one did.

"Why aren't you singing?" Asher murmured, and her eyes flew to his face. She hadn't realized he was awake.

"Because I'm writing down Bible verses."

"So... Are you done writing down Bible verses?"

"I guess I can be."

When they talked about taking him to the hospital, there was also the consideration that any movement was painful, and she wasn't even sure she would be able to get him in the truck.

Even now, after remembering how bad it hurt for him to just get into bed, she cringed at the idea of trying to get him in the vehicle. Of course, that had been a couple days ago, and every day, he seemed to be a little bit stronger, a little bit better.

"How about we sing something?"

"I don't know if I'll know all the words."

"I might be able to help you."

She huffed a laugh. "You can barely talk, you're not going to be able to sing. And if you do, it's going to hurt you."

"I think that's why it's called a sacrifice."

"What?"

"The Bible calls it a sacrifice of praise. I think when you have broken ribs, or whatever I have, and it hurts to sing, God likes to hear us anyway."

"If you say so, but I don't really think God takes pleasure in your pain."

"Not in my pain. My determination to praise Him even when it's hard."

"Oh."

That was an idea. She felt like she should write it down. That God wanted her to praise Him, even when it was hard. Or maybe, when she didn't want to, didn't feel like it, or wasn't sure it was going to help.

Maybe that's why Asher wanted her to sing. Because he thought it would help her.

"You know I'm doing better," she said.

"I know."

"No, really? You can tell?"

"Sure. You don't twist your fingers around as much, and you don't fidget quite as much as you had been."

It had only been a few days, but she pretty much spent all of her waking hours next to his bedside, unless she was doing one of the tasks that needed to be done. The fire had gone out, and there was only a tiny bit of firewood left, maybe enough to cook one meal, and she didn't have any wood to make more, and while he had offered to teach her how to use the chainsaw, she knew it was going to be verbal instruction only, and the chainsaw really did scare her. She had told him that she would rather be alive and a little bit chilly than toasty warm and dead.

He had laughed, and he hadn't insisted again. Maybe he had been thinking about the branch that had come down and hit him on the head. How he had almost died.

She would probably wonder for the rest of her life how close he had come to not waking up.

The thought scared her even now. And not so much because she would have been alone, but because...she'd found herself starting to care for him.

She looked over, surprised to find his eyes on her. "What?"

"Sing?"

"You're not back to those one-syllable sentences, are you?"

"No. And I might be up for something more than cream cheese today. Although, if my calculations are correct, we still have three and a half blocks left."

"Your calculations are indeed correct, except...I had some while you were sleeping so...three."

He snorted. He had taken to doing that rather than chuckling, because it was easier on his ribs.

"So... Do you think that you're going to be better before we run out of groceries?" It was a question that had been in the back of her mind. In fact, it was the question that had stirred the fear that had caused her to pick up her Bible and start writing down more verses.

"So you're asking me if I think we're going to starve to death?"

"Kind of." She supposed there wasn't much of a chance of that. And they weren't going to die of thirst, not with the creek right beside them, although she always used the sink for their drinking water. She hadn't asked where that water came from and assumed that it was safe to drink. If it wasn't, they didn't have any other choice, and she didn't want to know.

"No. I don't. I don't think we're going to starve to death, and I don't think anything terrible is going to happen to us. I think it's going to be a little bit before I can get up and on my feet, but that'll be fine, because I'm not eating as much as I would have been if I were healthy. Now, I do think we probably should cook that chicken in there before it goes bad. You think you can do it if I give you the instructions?"

"Sure." She started to put her notebook away.

"Seriously? I'm going to help you cook chicken, and you can't even sing to the man who almost died?"

She shook her head. She sang some in school and a little bit in church back when she went, but she hadn't sung for years, and it was kind of a novelty that he wanted her to do it and seemed to enjoy it.

"All right. I think I might be able to sing better than I can cook."

"I'm not only watching you. I'll help."

Maybe he was talking about both the cooking and the song, because she sang a little while before he joined in with some harmony, and she realized she liked it much better when he sang along.

I need Jesus, my need I now confess; No friend like Him in times of deep distress; I need Jesus, the need I gladly own; Though some may bear their load alone, Yet, I need Jesus.
I need Jesus, I need a friend like Him, A friend to guide when paths of life are dim; I need Jesus, when foes my soul assail; Alone I know I can but fail, So I need Jesus.
I need Jesus, I need Him to the end; No one like Him, He is the sinner's Friend; I need Jesus, no other friend will do; So constant, kind, so strong and true, Yes, I need Jesus.
I need Jesus, I need Jesus, I need Jesus every day; Need Him in the sunshine hour, Need Him when the storm-clouds lower; Every day along my way, Yes, I need Jesus.

Chapter Fifteen

Asher lay on his bed, frustrated. He couldn't even get up and go to the bathroom on his own, let alone cook for himself. He was trying to help Sondra as she cooked the chicken and made the topping to go with it. And it wasn't hard. She was doing okay, just fine...but he wanted to help her. Hated that he was sitting here, helpless, like a baby, or worse.

He had been excited at first, that they were going to be stuck together, thinking that he would have all this time to spend time with her and convince her that he was a guy she might be interested in. But if all he could do was lie in bed and throw up or pass out every time he tried to move, he was hardly going to convince her to look twice at him.

"Are you sure it's okay to use the last of the wood?" Sondra asked for the second time as she carried an armload from the emergency supplies he had behind the cabin.

"The later it gets in the spring, the less likely it's going to be that we have a cold night. If neither one of us have frozen to death the last three nights, I doubt it's going to happen now." Although from experience, he knew that the temperatures could dip pretty low unexpectedly, even in the middle of summer.

He wasn't going to worry about that, and he figured Sondra wasn't going to want to get up in the middle of the night and make a fire anyway.

She wouldn't want to face it, but probably the best thing that they could do would be to bundle up together and combine the blankets and their warmth.

Regardless, while it might get below freezing, he didn't think either one of them were in danger of freezing to death. They'd be uncomfortable, they'd be cold, tired, and miserable from not being able to sleep, but they wouldn't die.

She started working on the fire while he ran through his mind all of the different times he'd made the chicken.

"How did the chicken get its name?" she asked as she knelt by the stove.

"Ha. Well, one of my sisters, I think it was Lois, maybe, when she was like four or five, she looked at it sitting on her plate, and I guess she thought a piece of the spinach looked like a chicken eye somehow. So she asked Mom if there were chicken eyes in it. And before Mom could answer, Dad said, 'if there are, they're pretty sad,' you know, since they're dead, and all of us older kids laughed, but Claudia didn't really get it, and I think she actually thought Dad meant there *were* chicken eyes in it, so from then on, she called it Sad Eyes Chicken, and that just stuck. You know, the way your family has their own little quirks."

She made a noncommittal sound, and he remembered that her family really didn't have many quirks, not good ones, anyway.

He wanted to make her smile. She didn't have to be sad about her family for the rest of her life. "Just to be clear, there are no eyes in the recipe."

"That's a relief. You don't usually serve your guests anything with eyeballs in it, do you?"

"I do not."

He gave her some instructions, and she got started. The cabin also warmed up, and he hadn't realized how chilly it was. It was nice to have the wood to take the chill off, and he figured they'd better enjoy it, because he wasn't going to be cutting firewood for a while.

Although, he thought maybe he could sit up. He'd actually gotten pretty good at using the bedpan without getting out of bed, although it wasn't a talent he'd ever thought he was going to need.

However, Sondra hadn't had to wash any more blankets because of him, and he was grateful for that much, at least. He wasn't sure he'd ever been more embarrassed in his life, but he'd gotten used to her carrying the bedpan out for him and had stopped squirming every time he saw it.

While she was working on mixing up the spinach and cheese, he decided that he might as well try to sit up.

He rolled to his right side, which hurt less than his left, as he suspected there were no broken bones on it.

He was pretty sure at least one of his ribs were cracked, and maybe several, but he hadn't been able to feel where any were completely broken. Not that he spent a lot of time probing around, since even touching the skin hurt.

Still, he smothered a groan as his entire body protested the idea that he even think about moving.

But he didn't want to be bedbound any longer than he had to be. And moving around would be good for him. Even if it did hurt.

Remembering what had happened the last time he had moved, which was several days ago, and hopefully long enough that his body had healed a little more, he grabbed the bedpan just in case he had to throw up.

Taking a breath, trying to picture something that didn't feel like pain in his brain, he used his hands to push while he stretched forward and tried to sit up.

It felt like something dug a deep hole in his side, and he lost the ability to breathe for a moment. But he was able to get himself upright.

Just the change in posture alone made him dizzy, but the pain made it even worse.

He fumbled around for the bedpan as his stomach rebelled, and his throat squeezed.

He swallowed. He wouldn't throw up. He wasn't going to. He wouldn't allow himself. He didn't want Sondra to have that mess to deal with on top of everything else, although he should have stayed where he was, and then she wouldn't have to worry about it.

But he had to get up at some point. He couldn't lie around forever, and he didn't want to be so weak when he finally was able to get up that he couldn't do anything.

He sat on the edge of the bed.

"Asher? Did you hear me? Am I supposed to put—"

It sounded like Sondra had come to the doorway, but he was sitting on the other side of the bed and couldn't see.

"Asher Clybourn. What are you doing?"

It was a rhetorical question. His entire body was on fire from the pain, but he could recognize that at least.

"Did you throw up again?" she asked, and her words sounded snippy.

He couldn't blame her. He'd given her so much work to do. He wanted to take some of the burden off her, all of it, but he could hardly do that when he couldn't even stand up.

"So now you're not talking to me?" She came around the side of the bed and leaned over, looking in the bedpan. Then she took it from his fingers. "I can't leave you alone for a second, can I?"

"I'm sick of you doing all the work. I'm sick of being a burden on you. It wasn't supposed to be like this."

"It wasn't?"

He closed his eyes, his head still down. What had he said? Nothing that gave anything away. "No. You're not supposed to come to my cabin and wait on me hand and foot, change my blanket and sheets, and empty my bedpan. I can't even unbuckle my jeans by myself."

He closed his mouth, pressing his lips together tight. He wanted to stay positive. He wanted to look on the bright side, he wanted to continue to be upbeat, but the fact of the matter was, he was frustrated.

"Asher," Sondra said, and suddenly she was kneeling in front of him, her hand on his leg, trying to look up into his eyes.

He saw her blonde hair out of his peripheral vision, and if he could have moved, he would have put his hand over hers. As it was, he didn't want to ever move again, although this position was going to hurt until he lay back down. Even then, it was going to hurt for a while. Probably for an hour or two, if it ever quit.

He was tired of the pain, for sure, but that was secondary to the fact that he hated that he was so weak and inept in front of Sondra. He had wanted to make a good impression, and this certainly was not doing it.

"Asher. I'm sorry I got snippy." Her fingers rubbed gently over his knee, a light touch and one he appreciated. It seemed like everything that happened to him hurt, but that was one area on his body that didn't.

He moved his eyes to her face. The scratches had healed some, but they were still a testament to the fact that she had gotten hurt because of him.

He had found that the ones on her arms were even deeper and worse. She had laughingly said she had sat down on a thorn, and he hoped that she'd been able to get it pulled out, and it didn't get infected. He hadn't suggested he look at it, because he supposed that could definitely be taken the wrong way, but there was the chance that it hadn't gotten pulled out. Although, if it still bothered her, she didn't say. He was just so frustrated all the way around.

"No need to apologize."

"But I made you angry."

"No. I'm mad at myself."

"We just have to be patient. You'll heal eventually."

"I'm just frustrated."

"Because your healing is going slowly?" she asked, sounding uncertain.

He really didn't want to talk about it. He didn't want to explain in minute detail how helpless and stupid and frustrated he felt. How he didn't want her waiting on him hand and foot. How he wanted to be able to take care of her, not depend on her to take care of him.

He got mad just thinking about it, but she wasn't there for him to take his anger out on her either.

Pressing his lips together, he pursed them, trying to think of how he could explain it.

"Asher? Is there something more wrong? I mean, you seem... agitated."

"I'm frustrated. I don't want you to have to take care of me. It's supposed to be me taking care of you. And yet, it hurts to pretty much do anything. I can't even stand up. Can't go to the bathroom myself. I... I can't fix anything, can't do any more, and—"

"Did it ever occur to you that I'm enjoying this?"

"What?" He lifted his head enough to look into her eyes. She was sincere. Had he heard her correctly?

"It's only been a few days... I haven't minded."

"Did you remember that I peed on the blankets? And you had to wash them? That you have to take my pee out of the house every day? That I stink?"

"Well, I can give you a bath, if you want, such as it is. But I think I stink too. I've been wearing these clothes for four days, and I feel really filthy, and I guess if I think about it, I could get frustrated about that, but really, you've done me a favor."

"Because I helped you learn that you can live in dirty clothes?"

"No, silly. Because... I started to read the Bible. I... I'm actually using the outhouse, even though I know that there is a raccoon above my head during the day, and in the evening, I try to be careful that I don't catch her on her way out. She has five babies. Did I tell you that?"

"I think I remember you saying something about a raccoon. In the outhouse?"

"On the rafters. I figured out there must be a small spot up there, and she and her five babies are up there."

"Kits. Baby raccoons are called kits."

"Kits. She and her kits are up there." She smiled, as though she liked that. Her hand rubbed over his leg again. And her eyes searched his face. "I mean, do you remember the first time I used it?"

"Not really. I had to have my fingers in my ears, remember?" He didn't really feel like making a joke, but he did anyway and was rewarded with her laughter.

"Exactly. Now, while I am careful about how I open the door, and I step in carefully as well, because the raccoon and I are not exactly...what you would call friends. Just kind of acquaintances."

"All right."

"Anyway, sometimes I go down in the evening just so I can see her and her babies go out. They do it right around dusk. And as I'm sitting there waiting for them, I'm listening like you told me to. And watching, and...smelling. It smells different by the creek than it does over on the other side of the clearing, where I found you."

"It always smells different beside the water. Also, on that side of the cabin, there are a bunch of pine trees, whereas on the other side, they're mostly oak."

"See, I couldn't tell what the difference was from, but I knew there was a difference."

"Yeah. That's kind of impressive."

"And last night, I don't know if you noticed, you were pretty sore and tired when I gave you your pain pill." They'd taken to giving him one before he went to bed. Sometimes it upset his stomach, but it helped him sleep. "I walked outside on the porch. It was cold, I borrowed your jacket, I hope that was okay."

"Anything in here that's mine is yours." He meant it. He'd give her anything.

"Thanks. But I didn't even ask, because I remembered what you said. And after reading my Bible a little, I guess I... I just felt like I wanted to go out and see for myself. Listen. And while there were some sounds that were a little bit scary, the howling wolf sounded a lot closer last night than it did the night you were with me, I knew I could step in the cabin anytime. And the stars were beautiful. The wind refreshing. I hardly recognize myself sometimes and can't believe it's only been a few days."

"I'm sure you'd like to go home."

Chapter Sixteen

One side of Asher's mouth pulled back, and he said that with a mixture of sadness and disgust. No one wanted to be forced to stay somewhere against their will.

"I don't know. I mean, yeah. I guess. But it took about twenty-four hours before I stopped feeling like I needed to reach for my phone every two minutes. And after that, especially every time I got scared, I would either read your Bible or read the notebook where I'd written down the verses that I thought would help me. And you know, the verses on fear are really good. But the things that really help me during the day are the praise verses, where you start thinking about how wonderful God is, and that kind of takes my mind off the things that make me anxious."

"Diversion. That's a smart tactic."

"Well, I guess it has a name, although I hadn't really been thinking about it that way. It's just, God's way works, I guess. And I've never really given it a chance before. I'd always used TV and electronics and people to make me feel better. But God wants to. If I just allow Him."

He nodded. Still frustrated, but she had just said so much that had eased his heart and mind.

"It's good to know that you feel like this has been a benefit to you, because I honestly didn't expect to come here and have you doing everything. Including taking care of me."

"I know you didn't. I know you didn't have that branch fall on top of you on purpose. I know you didn't put yourself through this kind of pain just to torture me or whatever. You don't think I believe that for one second, do you?"

He thought about how he had wanted to have her there, for himself. Because he liked her. How he thought that he might get her to notice him, that they might develop something between them. He certainly had had ulterior motives, although he hadn't injured himself on purpose.

"I suppose that man is wicked and capable of pretty much anything."

"Are you saying you hurt yourself on purpose?" The tone of her voice changed, and it held disbelief and concern.

"No. No, I didn't. I mean, I don't really remember the few minutes before the tree hit me, but I don't have any memory of having any plans to hurt myself. And if I had known it would hurt this much, I would definitely have told myself to forget about it."

She laughed a little, and he smiled along with her.

"So...are you going to try to lie back down?"

"No. I was going to sit here until the pain eases up a little, then stand up."

"Asher. You think that's a good idea?"

"I don't care."

She sighed, sounding a little put out. "You do realize that if you fall down, or black out, or throw up, I'm going to be the one cleaning up the mess."

"I know. I'm going to do my best not to do any of those things, because I don't want to put any more burden on you."

"Then how about you just lie back down? And then, it won't be a burden for either one of us."

"I'm not going to get any stronger if I just lie around in bed."

"Has anyone ever told you that you are extremely stubborn?"

"I prefer to think of myself as determined," he said, and he stuck his nose in the air just a little, although he wasn't feeling the whole teasing/flirting thing.

Wait, was he flirting?

"Stubborn, determined." She sighed. "I suppose determined is the positive spin of stubborn, but I still think you're stubborn. Because I think you need to get a little bit better before you start trying to stand up."

She might have been right.

But he didn't want to wait. Although the idea of more pain was something that he really didn't want to face, pain was less odious to him than staying in bed was.

"All right. Tell me how I can help you," she said, and while she didn't sound overly happy, she didn't sound angry either.

"Just let me stand up. Even if it's for a couple of seconds. I promise, I'll try not to make any messes on your floor. And if I make a mess, I'll clean it up."

She laughed. "Sure. You'll clean it up...a couple weeks from now when you're actually able to do things, and until then I'm going to have to smell it. So no. Thank you for the offer, but any messes will get cleaned up by me, today."

"I didn't realize you were so particular," he said, giving her a look.

"And I didn't realize you were so handsome." Her eyes got big, and she slapped a hand over her mouth. "I didn't mean to say that. I meant stubborn. Yeah. Stubborn."

"No. You said handsome."

All right. That was worth all the pain that he had gone through. If she meant it. Unless it really was some kind of weird slip that she actually didn't mean. But from the way her cheeks were heating up and the way her eyes had flown open, maybe she had thought that a time or two.

"All right," she said. "I like the stubble. It...makes you look rugged. Rough in a way that is not off putting. Handsome. Okay? That's it. I just, you know, have a thing for beards or whatever." She shrugged, like it wasn't any big deal, and then said, "Now, are you getting up, or am I going to shove you back down on that bed and tie you up."

He thought that maybe she didn't realize exactly how that was going to sound until it came out, and although she'd been really adorable when she was embarrassed about the last thing that she said, he decided he wasn't going to tease her about that. It would be funny, but it wasn't really his thing anyway.

So, they both ignored that, just pretended she meant exactly what it sounded like she meant, which was probably exactly what she meant, although it wasn't the image that had been in his brain.

"My right side doesn't hurt as much, and I can use that arm without as much pain. So, that might be a good side for you to be on."

"Although if you're going to fall, it would be the best side to fall on."

He couldn't even imagine how much it would hurt if he actually fell. Hopefully he passed out.

"Yeah. So, if I look like I'm going to go, just give me a pull."

"All right. If the guy's gonna pass out, yank down. That seems...a little bit mean, but if you insist."

"I insist. I think we'll both be better off if that happens."

But he had no intention of falling down. He was going to stand up, then he'd give himself a break for a little bit, but he'd try to get up later too. He might as well. Surely if he was in the hospital, they wouldn't allow him to just lie around, but they'd force him up. Of course, they probably also had stronger pain meds.

"All right. You ready?" He looked up at her. Suddenly thinking about what she had said. He was handsome. She liked his beard. He was not going to forget that.

She nodded, and he had to take a minute to remind himself of what they were talking about. That's right, he was going to stand up.

Taking as deep of a breath as he could without making things hurt too much, he used his right hand to push off the bed while he willed his legs to straighten and take his weight.

The pain was excruciating, and his vision cracked, and he thought he really might pass out.

Thankfully, he didn't throw up, and he didn't fall on her. But he stood with his legs apart, like he was on the deck of a wildly tossing ship. Which was honestly how it felt.

He stood for two seconds, maybe four, but it was enough.

"Sitting," he said breathlessly.

That was the only word he got out of his mouth, but he didn't need to say anything more, because Sondra understood. She was there, but it didn't feel like she was hovering, and she had given him plenty of space.

He lowered himself slowly, with her taking a hold of his forearm and his hand, and he squeezed tightly, holding on and using her to balance.

He wanted to plop down, but he knew that that would jar his ribs and possibly make the pain even worse than it had been when he had been standing.

He breathed out as he sat down and slowly twisted, lying back down on his back.

It still hurt, but it was the least offensive of all of the positions he could be in.

He closed his eyes. He felt like sleeping for a week now.

"Are you okay?" Sondra asked, her hands still on his arm and her form hovering over him.

He cracked his eyes enough to see her before he closed them again.

"Yeah. Thanks. I know that was a stupid, little thing, but I just... I needed to do it." He couldn't really explain, any more than he couldn't stand to be laid up, and he felt like he needed to be working on getting his strength back. The only way to do that was to fight through the pain, and the weakness, and the nausea and make himself do it.

"I'm not entirely convinced that we shouldn't have taken you to the emergency room."

"Well, I'm pretty sure I'm totally convinced that I couldn't have made it to the pickup, and the ride down would have been the worst ride of my life. Easy."

"I can't argue with that. But at some point, I could have gone and used someone's phone. Called an ambulance, and that ride wouldn't have been quite so bad."

"Okay. Truly. I think if there was anything seriously wrong with me, we would have figured that out by now."

She didn't have an argument with that, and he appreciated that. It might be a crazy thing, but he would rather die in his cabin than spend any amount of time in the hospital. Not for this. Plus, he didn't want to give up this time with Sondra.

Maybe time would tell that he had made a foolish decision, but for now, he was content.

"All right. Now, are you going to help me with this chicken? Or are you going to try to do something else crazy while you think my back is turned?"

"We probably ought to get that chicken done before the fire goes out. That was the last of the wood, wasn't it?"

"It was." She bit her lip. "Do you think it's going to be a problem?"

"No. I don't."

"What aren't you telling me?" she asked, and he was surprised that she could read anything on his face. He thought he'd been pretty good at closing it off.

"I don't think we're going to freeze to death. It might drop down below freezing and get cold, and we might end up having to share body warmth and blankets, but I just don't think that not having a fire is the major problem that it would be if this were, say, January."

"All right. Although, sharing a bed with you when you hurt so much is not exactly my idea of a good time. I'll be petrified to even breathe."

"Well, I don't think it will come to that. Just the worst-case scenario."

She didn't say anything, and she almost looked...disappointed. Or upset. Maybe at the idea that he had said that her having to share a bed with him was the worst-case scenario?

Surely not. He could hardly believe that she was beginning to feel affection for him. How could she? But she'd called him handsome, and now she seemed...almost upset that they weren't going to end up having to share a bed.

Maybe he was reading her all wrong. He wasn't exactly known for being an expert on women. Far from it. But he could consider himself encouraged anyway.

She walked back out of the bedroom and into the kitchen, and he watched as she moved around it. Her movements seemed graceful, and there was almost a liquid smoothness about her motions that he couldn't help admire.

Maybe all women moved like that, but he only ever noticed it in

Sondra. Maybe it was true what she'd said about her carrying some extra weight around her waist and hips. But...it made her soft. Gave her a softness that made her feel more approachable to him. Not in a she wasn't as good as someone else so he wasn't as intimidated way but more of a she was human and very attractive kind of way.

He wasn't sure how to explain it, and he closed his eyes so she wouldn't catch him staring.

She called out a question about the chicken, how to cook it in the woodstove, and he answered her, still thinking about the way she moved, and the way she felt, and the way she had been taking care of him.

She hardly talked about her shows at all, and she seemed more interested in learning more about what the Bible said.

Maybe, maybe this really was going to be the best thing that could have happened to both of them.

<h1 style="text-align:center">Chapter Seventeen</h1>

A week later, Sondra stood in the kitchen, prepping the last of the groceries they'd bought when they first arrived. She almost felt like a completely different person than the one who had arrived at the cabin.

She no longer thought about checking her phone. Every once in a while, she wondered what was going on with her social media accounts, but she hardly ever longed to catch one of her shows.

It was amazing to her what could happen to a person when they were taken away from everything and dropped in the middle of nowhere.

She looked at the food around her, some carrots, celery, the last of the chicken, and a block of cream cheese. The last one.

If someone would have told her that she was going to buy eight blocks of cream cheese and use every single one of them in less than two weeks, she would have told them they were nuts.

But that had happened.

She tried not to worry about what they were going to eat once this was all gone.

She mentioned to Asher the previous day that they had one more day of vegetables, and he nodded, but they hadn't talked about it anymore.

He'd insisted on getting out of bed every day since the first day he got up. Each day, he got out and stood. A couple of days, he had taken a few steps, and yesterday, he walked the whole way to the kitchen.

Still, she didn't think he was up to an hour-long drive to town, and...they were out of food.

She glanced at the notebook that was never far from her.

What time I am afraid, I will trust in thee.
But my God shall supply all your need according to his riches in glory by Christ Jesus.

Lord, help me not to be afraid.

It had become obvious to her over the last week that her TV shows were cover for her fear. When she sank into them, she didn't have to think about all the scary things that were happening in her life, and the media filled the empty place inside of her, giving her a false sense of calm and security when she fell into those fictional worlds. The same thing could have been true for her with books, if she'd been a reader. Just, the characters felt real, and their stories gave her something to occupy her mind, rather than tinkering with the worries that always seemed to be on the very edge of her consciousness, occasionally taking over.

Not that she thought that there was anything wrong with watching TV, or reading books for that matter, but she'd used them in place of the Lord. Used them as a balm for her anxiety, instead of turning to God.

They weren't a very good fix. Just something temporary that took her mind off her troubles.

Which again, wasn't a terrible thing, except they had become an idol to her, because she had filled her spare time with TV and social media rather than having a real life.

She regretted the wasted years. The wasted time. The time that she could have been doing something to help others, and instead, she grasped at everything Hollywood put out, trying to soothe her soul.

She finished chopping the carrot and grabbed another one. She had no idea what she was making, just using the last of their ingredients and putting them all together. She was the picky one. Asher would eat anything. He hadn't complained about a single thing she set in front of him, and a couple of the things she made had been rather iffy.

Actually, yesterday, when he'd come out to the kitchen, he hadn't said anything, but he just picked something up and started helping her.

It wasn't quite as fun as the night in the grocery store, since the man was still in pain. A lot of it. But Asher was the kind of person she wanted to be—always looking on the bright side, always content, ready with a joke, a smile, and seemed to find enjoyment in the smallest things, and she really enjoyed their time together.

"Hey there."

She looked up in surprise to see Asher standing in the doorway, one shoulder leaning against the doorjamb, his eyes dark, but a small smile playing around his lips where his stubble had turned into an honest-to-goodness beard.

It was the perfect length in her opinion, and every time she looked at it, her heart skipped a bit.

Or maybe it was Asher, not the beard.

She hid her disconcert with bluster. "What are you doing out of bed? I thought we agreed that if you were going to get up, you were going to have me there, in case you passed out."

"Or in case I threw up, so you could catch it and not have a mess all over the place."

"That too." She put a hand on her hip and gave him her best schoolmarm look. "How am I supposed to get anything done if all I do is keep an eye on you to make sure that you haven't decided all the sudden that you're going to get up and make a pilgrimage to Alaska or something?"

"I don't think you have to worry about that today. Maybe tomorrow."

"Well, maybe we could go to town to get groceries instead of traveling the whole way to Alaska."

She just assumed that she was going to go with him whenever he went, and he didn't correct her. It wasn't like he was keeping her here against her will. Although, she certainly hadn't expected to live in the same clothes for seven days when they'd left Sweet View Ranch in North Dakota.

Asher had given her full access to the clothes he had, but he only had a few extras, and they were way too big for her. She wore his clothes while she washed hers and waited for them to dry, which took an entire day, since they had no dryer. And it was up to her to wring all the extra water out, and her jeans especially just took time to dry.

She managed to scour around the woods and pick up enough dead branches to keep the stove heated every day to cook. She tried to do it in the evening, so it would keep the house warm for a little bit at night.

She had had no idea how much wood it took just to make a fire to cook with. And she guarded her small store very judiciously, putting it out as soon as she was done cooking, because finding wood was not easy.

Other than that, it really hadn't been terrible. She...actually enjoyed their time away. And sitting out on the porch step in the evening was one of her favorite things to do.

"I thought I might make the fire for you today," he said as he took a couple of slow steps into the kitchen.

"Well. Are you sure you're up to it?" It was almost funny to think she still found things to be afraid of. She was petrified that he was going to pass out, hurt himself more, and she would end up stuck here even longer.

They figured out that his key had fallen out of the pocket of his jeans somehow, and she searched the yard and found it eventually. So she did have access to his pickup, but the idea of driving that thing down the winding mountain road, and trying to find a house, made her hunt for her notebook so she could say a couple of verses, which helped calm her fear.

She actually didn't need her notebook much anymore. She said some of the verses so much that she had many of them memorized. She actually memorized the entire Psalm 91.

"Well, I guess I won't know until I try." He grinned at her, although he winced immediately.

Any major movement hurt him still. And he tried to be sparing with the pain pills. She had figured that he ought to use as many as he needed, but he said that he didn't want to run out, just in case something happened.

And she understood what he meant. Perhaps he would fall down, or probably what he was really thinking was she might need them. She found that he was as considerate as a person could be to her. Always making sure that he made things as easy as he could for her. Even though he was mostly housebound and in bed.

"I'm not sure I feel like picking you up off the floor today, so be careful, okay?" Her words were a little harsh, but her tone was soft. She really didn't want him up, but she knew the only way he was going to get his strength back was to do a little more each day.

She just hated to see him hurting.

It was kind of funny how fond she'd become of him.

He walked carefully over to the stove and knelt down before it.

She kept the box of matches he had sitting on the little metal lip in front of it. That way she didn't have to look for them when it was time to light the fire.

She'd actually taken to watching the sun come up over the mountain in the morning and loved that time almost as much as she enjoyed watching it go down. Those were the best times for her to sit and read her Bible and, as Asher had suggested, listen to nature.

He knelt down, and she watched as she finished chopping the vegetables as he worked carefully, striking a match after adjusting the small amount of wood in the stove so that it would catch quickly and burn as long as possible.

He taught her a little bit about making fires from his bed, before he could get up, and then after he'd come out, sometimes he talked while he was working. But today, he was quiet.

The kindling she had inside caught, and he stood gingerly, his face twisting as he straightened, and grabbed the box of matches.

He took it and set it on the counter where he kept it while the stove was hot.

"I was thinking we would go down the mountain tomorrow. I... I'm not sure I'm up to an eight-hour drive to get home, but I can try if that's what you want."

Her eyes brightened immediately. She could go home! She could... get clean clothes. Catch up on all the latest, have her phone charged again.

But as she looked at him, she knew he wasn't quite ready for that. Although, she believed him when he said he would do it for her.

"We could just get groceries and come back?"

"Yeah. There's probably not a store in that town where you can buy any kind of clothing, although I'm guessing you'd really like it if we could."

"Oh my goodness. Yes. I don't think I'm ever going to wear these clothes again. I'll probably throw them away when we get home."

"That's actually my favorite outfit," he said, glancing at her, and there was something in his eyes that made her body heat a little. It was an odd sensation, and her fingers flew to her chest, and she was at a loss for words, for once.

She knew he was being silly, since it was her only outfit, but as her eyes raised to meet his, there was something in them that...made her heart flutter.

"This is my only outfit," she finally managed to say, but her voice was softer and didn't hold its usual bluster.

His lips curved up slowly, and her fingers curled. "I know. Good thing it's my favorite."

"I am not dressing to impress you. I'm dressing for function, not fashion."

"I think that's probably wise around here," he said, and then he turned and started shuffling toward the door.

"Where are you going?"

"There is no wood in the box. I thought I'd go see if I could find some."

"You haven't been outside in a week. Now all of a sudden, you're going to go scrounging for wood?"

"Needs to be done."

Chapter Eighteen

Sometimes Sondra wanted to throttle Asher. Didn't he know if something happened to him, she was going to be devastated?

Because she would be stranded up here alone, not because she cared overly much for him, she added swiftly to herself, although the more time she spent with him, the less accurate that was. If she were being honest, she had started to care for him, way more than what she should.

"Fine. I'll go with you." Most of the vegetables were chopped, and she was just waiting for the stove to get hot so she could cook them.

She supposed she'd boil them, then add the cream cheese and a couple of spices. She really didn't have a set recipe in mind, just using up the last of the groceries.

"I love it. I'll find the wood, and you can carry it."

"My eyes are just as good as yours, and I have no pain. Why don't you sit here and watch the fire that you just started, and I'll go find wood for us?"

"Nope. I'm going to get some. You can come if you want to, or you can stay."

His words were not angry, but they were firm. Ever since he'd basically told her that he couldn't stand not being able to do anything and had gotten upset and frustrated that one day, he'd been much more in control.

She didn't think the anger and frustration were gone necessarily, but it was like her fear, he had been taking it to the Lord and dealing with it that way.

"Asher, wait." She hurried toward him as he stepped carefully out of the door, holding on to the doorframe with his right hand.

He ignored her as he continued moving forward.

He was panting when she reached him, and she figured there was no way he was going to walk around the yard, let alone go to the woods and carry anything back.

But if there was one thing she learned about him in the last week or so, it was that he could be very determined and extremely stubborn.

While at times those qualities made her want to beat her head against the wall, she also admired them in him. He didn't let things stop him. He worked hard once he figured out what he wanted to do. And she admired that. Because she wasn't necessarily like that.

She...got discouraged easily and quit when things got hard. That had been the story of her life. The only thing she'd really been successful in was getting and keeping her website designing business. And even then, when she had a client who was hard to please, she was much more likely to turn her computer off and sit on the couch binge-watching a season of her latest show than she was to knuckle down and dig into the work.

"Please. Let me help you." She tried to modulate her voice as she closed the door and stood beside him at the top of the steps.

His right hand held the railing, and he stood studying the three steps, like they were Mount Everest. And he was about to climb to the top.

"Let me stand over there, and you can put your arm around me, and I'll help you."

She didn't know if it was a good idea for him to go down the steps, because once she got him down, she had to get him back up.

Except, it wasn't her. It was him. He would have to get himself back up, although of course she would help.

"Let me go down. And then..." He grunted a little. "I think I'll need help getting back up."

"You read my mind." She stepped back and, on one hand, wanted to close her eyes, but on the other, she needed to see what was going to happen.

He went slowly, gripping the railing, and while she couldn't see his face because she was standing behind him, she could only imagine it was scrunched up tight.

She couldn't fathom how painful it must be, although she knew the pain wasn't nearly as bad now as it had been. If she had broken her ribs, she would have lain in bed until there wasn't the slightest twinge of pain. She certainly wouldn't have gotten up to face it every day. She also would have downed the entire bottle of pain pills and not worried about keeping any back in case someone else needed them.

Just those two things made her admire Asher, for his foresight, his determination, and his consideration.

She certainly didn't think of him as "that kid" anymore.

He made it down the first two steps and then paused. Then, she could see him shaking as he lowered himself the last little bit and stood on the ground. She let out the breath she'd been holding, and hurried down, but stood back, because she didn't want to overwhelm him. She knew she had a tendency to be...hovering, and while he didn't seem to mind, she figured it was probably annoying.

"Wow. I wasn't sure you were going to make it."

"That makes two of us," he said. "I think... I think I'm going to sit down for a bit. I feel bad, I started the fire inside, and I don't have anything to put on it."

"If you're going to sit there, I can scrounge around. I found a bunch this morning, and I didn't carry it all back. It looked like maybe you had cut some a few winters ago and forgot about it or something."

"I think it might have snowed, and I hadn't gotten it all carried back. I forgot about that. But I suppose that's good now."

She nodded her head and then said, "Are you going to stay there? Seriously, Asher. I don't want anything to happen to you. And not just because it's going to make more work for me." They'd been joking about that the whole week. But it was true, anything that happened to him was going to affect her.

"I'll stay. Like a good dog." He smiled, but there wasn't much humor on his face. And she could tell he was frustrated again. He wanted his recovery to go faster.

She was tempted to pat him on the head, but she didn't.

"I don't have any doggy treats, but if you'll take an IOU, I can give you some later."

"No treats? Then forget it."

"If we go to the store tomorrow, I can grab some," she said, happy that he seemed to be coming out of his morose mood and able to joke a little.

"No. Dogs don't remember from one day to the other. If you're going to reward me, it has to be immediate."

"All right. I'll scratch your ears if you're still there when I get back."

"Kiss me, and you've got yourself a deal."

Her eyes widened and flew to his, but she couldn't read his face to tell whether he was joking or serious. His eyes just stared at her, and there wasn't a glimpse of his smile. He didn't look like he wished he could take the words back, but he didn't look like he was begging for her to accept, either.

It was like he just said *how about you give me a carrot when you come back*. And not something so personal.

"All right. If it will keep you on that step, you got it."

He had to have been joking. He couldn't possibly want to kiss her. For goodness' sake, she was wearing the same clothes she had been wearing last week this time. And she'd been fixing her hair with no mirror and no brush either. Just throwing a little water on it, making sure it wasn't sticking up at odd angles.

He couldn't possibly find her attractive.

Why would he have said that?

She worried the question over in her head as she walked directly to the place where she'd been that morning and saw the pieces that were half buried in forest litter.

Was he bored? Was it his idea of getting some excitement in his life? Was he just trying to embarrass her?

Maybe she would get back and he would say that he had just been kidding. Or maybe he was talking about a kiss to the forehead.

As soon as she thought that, she wanted to slap her own forehead. Of course. He wasn't talking about a real kiss. He was talking about a forehead kiss. Something that a friend might drop on another friend's forehead. That was it. The kind of kiss you gave your dog. Yeah. Because they were talking about dogs.

She felt like a fool for even considering that there might have been something more in his statement, and to her surprise, she was disappointed.

What was that about?

Although, she had been admiring him for the last week and a half. Not just his determination and his stubbornness, and his consideration, but he had confidence, he knew what he was doing. He didn't sit around twiddling his thumbs and worrying. Not the way she did. Although she was working on it, and she thought she was getting better. But he had a quiet self-assurance that he would be able to do what he set out to do.

Maybe that was why he was so frustrated with himself when his body didn't cooperate.

But even so, he only had that one time where he'd gotten visibly upset.

She came back with enough firewood to last through supper, and she even thought it might heat the stove for breakfast if they put it out as soon as she was done cooking.

Sure enough, Asher still sat on the bottom step.

She couldn't believe the relief that she felt, and it had nothing to do with him not getting hurt and everything to do with her being concerned that he was teasing her about wanting to kiss her and was going to disappear so he didn't have to.

Maybe it was a relief, maybe it was...a bit of eagerness, mixed with excitement.

"I really didn't expect you to still be here," she said, stopping for a second in front of him.

"I'd sit here all day, for that kind of reward."

Was he talking about the kiss? Her eyes widened, and to her surprise, she was breathless.

"I'm gonna take these things up and put them in the woodbox, and then I'll be back, okay?"

"I'll be here. Waiting. You promised."

He glanced up at her, and there was a bit of twinkle in his eye, but there was also a seriousness that she could not mistake.

It made her knees weak.

She turned and went up the steps, wondering if she was reading him all wrong. But she supposed she'd find out. Because she absolutely was going back down the steps, and she was going to play this out until the end.

Setting the wood in the box, she grabbed one piece, the smallest, and opened up the stove, throwing it on top of the kindling that had caught and was burning nicely. Looking at herself, covered in the litter from the woods and with pieces of rotten wood sticking to her clothes and her hands filthy, she couldn't believe she was going to go back outside and hope that some man was going to kiss her.

No. Not "some man." Asher. She hoped that Asher was going to kiss her.

She could hardly brush herself off inside, so she hurried out the door and down the steps.

Asher had stood up, and he gingerly turned as she descended, brushing her shirt off as unobtrusively as possible and then rubbing her hands together to get the worst of it off.

"I'm a mess," she said, like he couldn't see that with his own eyes.

"That's not what I see," he said. But he didn't say anything more, and she wasn't quite sure what he meant.

Standing had made him breathless, and his right hand still held onto the railing as he shifted a bit toward her.

"I'm waiting for my reward," he murmured. Still out of breath.

"Well, you're going to have to lean down a little so I can give it to you." She tried to pretend she wasn't discombobulated and nervous and terrified and excited and a little scared.

She hadn't considered until just that very moment, but this could change their relationship. It could mess up the easy camaraderie that had fallen between them, or it could shift things in a different direction.

Or if he kissed her the way she might kiss her dog, nothing would have to change, although her heart would definitely be sad about that.

"So, do you want it on your forehead or your cheek?" she asked, thinking that if she kissed his cheek, she would be kissing his beard.

He lifted his left hand, and there was a little tightening around his eyes that said it still hurt to move as he took one finger and pointed toward his lips.

He didn't say anything, just stared at her.

"All right."

She swallowed and tried to pretend her stomach wasn't writhing and her throat wasn't tight.

She put a hand on his right side and lifted her face. Even standing on her toes, she couldn't quite reach, and she murmured, "I need you to bend down."

Their eyes met, and he held her gaze as he bent closer.

That made her even more nervous, but she couldn't look away, until his face was so close she could no longer see it, and then she took her hand and put it carefully around his neck to steady herself as she looked up again and pressed her lips to his.

That was all it was, but her breath caught, and her body froze, and she didn't move, and neither did he.

She hadn't been sure what she was planning on doing, but it wasn't standing there, with her lips pressed to his, not moving. Long moments went by. She supposed they did anyway, she wasn't really thinking about time, she was thinking about more. She was thinking about being closer. About being surprised, not expecting to not be able to just brush her lips to his and step back, laughing. She wanted to move closer, wanted to deepen the kiss, have it last longer.

She wasn't expecting it to affect her like it did either. She was incapable of laughing it off as they moved apart, just enough to look into each other's eyes.

He didn't seem the slightest bit surprised. Although, his eyelids were lowered a little and his breath was ragged. Of course, that could be because he wasn't used to standing up, and it might have nothing to do with kissing her.

It must've been ten or fifteen heartbeats where they stood there, both of their chests going up and down, their eyes entangled, until she broke her gaze away and ran up the steps, calling over her shoulder, "I'm getting supper on the stove."

She closed the door behind her and went over to the table, putting her hands on it and leaning her weight on that piece of furniture because her knees were shaking. Why? Why in the world was she so... undone, over what should have been a very simple kiss?

What had happened just then? And what did it mean?

She had no answers, and she didn't know how she was going to face him when he walked in the door. Because there was no way she could deny that his kiss had been wildly more than what she expected, and she didn't think there was any way she could pretend it hadn't been.

Chapter Nineteen

Asher stood at the foot of the stairs, cursing his weakness, his inability to do anything more than hobble around, and that very slowly. He couldn't even grab her to him and hold her tight the way he wanted to. Because movement on his left side felt like a knife being stabbed into his heart, and he needed his right hand to hold onto the railing and balance.

It figures, after a decade of crushing on her in secret, he finally, finally got the kiss that he dreamed about, and all he could do was pant and look into her eyes and wish that he was strong enough to hold her close and had the air to murmur all the things he wanted to tell her, all the words she deserved to hear.

But maybe that was for the best, because it seemed like kissing him had upset her. If her running away was any indication.

He hadn't kissed a lot of girls, but he'd never had one rush off like he disgusted her so much she couldn't wait to go in and wash her face or whatever. He didn't even know.

He took his right hand off the banister long enough to run it through his hair and over his beard, which had grown longer than he normally allowed it to. He didn't typically keep his face completely clean-shaven, but he didn't normally have a bunch of hair growing on it either. It was itchy, although it kept him warm in the winter.

He took as deep a breath as his ribs would allow and blew it out. He could feel the throbbing in his temple which indicated another headache was coming on. He'd dealt with them since the accident. Sometimes they were so bad he could hardly stand it. That's when he would take a pain pill. Honestly, the headaches almost bothered him more than the sore ribs.

He felt throbbing from the top of his head the whole way down his knees; sometimes his legs hurt if it was a really bad one.

This felt like that kind, but he should go inside, help with supper, do something to take some of the burden off Sondra.

She'd changed while they were there, and he thought that maybe she was eager to go home, to get away from him, to stop serving him every hour of the day.

He wasn't used to being weak, wasn't used to lying around, and definitely wasn't used to having someone wait on him hand and foot.

He stood for just a little bit more, wondering if he was actually going to have the stamina to go down the mountain and get groceries. Sondra hadn't said, but he knew she was worried about the food situation.

For him, he knew they'd be fine for another week or so, even if they didn't have any food. They had water, and plenty of it, and they'd be fine. Hungry, but fine.

But he didn't want to do that to Sondra. And with no food, he would have a lot harder time getting his strength back.

Sondra had made sure that he at least got his calories in, finding creative ways to serve him the cream cheese. She gave it to him with honey, with some spices that he wasn't sure exactly what they were sprinkled over the top of it, and he had to admit that was really good. She put it on toast and served it in pretty much every meal they had.

He wasn't sure whether it was the cream cheese or not, but he hadn't lost as much weight as he would have expected to, and he credited Sondra for that.

Actually, Sondra deserved the credit for everything. He might have died if she hadn't been there with him.

The thought didn't scare him so much, because he knew the timing was all God. After all, God knew when he was there alone, and God knew that this time he had Sondra, so this was the time that the branch had come down.

And yeah, he believed that God controlled everything. Every little thing. The Bible clearly said that all the hairs on his head were numbered. If God went down to that small of a detail, God certainly could tell whether or not a branch was going to fall from a tree.

And He could keep it up until He was ready for it to fall at that exact moment Asher was under it.

When he thought of all the weeks that he'd been there, and how he'd chosen that exact spot in the woods to work, and he hadn't even started his chainsaw, it was definitely the Lord who had all that in His plan.

Anyway, if it would have been God's plan for it to fall on him while he had been there alone, he probably wouldn't have made it. Sondra had made sure, dragged him when she needed to, kicking and screaming at times it seemed like, to getting healthy again.

He owed her a lot, and he probably shouldn't have asked for that kiss. He hadn't been able to believe it when the words came out of his mouth. What had he been thinking?

But she'd done it. She kissed him.

He half expected her to drop a kiss on his forehead when she went by him, which is the reason he'd stood up. Well, part of it. He hadn't wanted to kiss her sitting down. He'd wanted to be able to hold her, to kiss her the way he dreamed about for so long.

Of course, that hadn't happened. He'd practically been panting in her face, unable to catch his breath, and it was only partly because of his injuries.

It was mostly because the woman he'd been dreaming about for so long was finally standing in front of him, lifting her sweet face up and allowing him to kiss her.

His hand tightened on the banister, and he wanted to knock his forehead against it, which would do nothing for the headache that was spiking in his temple. But it would relieve some of his frustration. Frustration that he had an opportunity, but he couldn't take it, all he could do was...kiss her like he was in kindergarten.

Man. She already saw him as a little kid, and now she figured he kissed like one too.

He blew out a breath, then figured there was no point in standing there and castigating himself more. He was going to have to face her at some point, and he didn't have the energy or the ability to stomp off across the yard and go chop down a tree or cut firewood or something. Something to burn off his frustration.

So, he turned around, grasping the other banister with his right hand and carefully moving up the steps, resting at the top as he wobbled a bit and his vision blackened before it cleared.

He hated this weakness, hated that he couldn't do what he wanted to do, hated that he was at the mercy of someone else.

The only thing he didn't hate was that it was Sondra, and she kissed him, and that almost made everything else worthwhile.

Chapter Twenty

Asher walked into the cabin, closing the door carefully behind him. Sondra did not look up from where she knelt in front of the stove, poking it with the metal poker that he kept leaning against the wall behind it.

Whatever she had made for supper was on the stove, and he could see the ever-loving block of cream cheese sitting on the counter, opened and cut into pieces.

He closed the door carefully behind him, trying to ignore the shooting pain in his head and the stabbing pain in his side.

It almost seemed like she was mad at him.

Was that a dirty trick? He didn't make her kiss him. She could have chosen not to. He hadn't really been serious when he first said it.

Would his foolishness destroy the friendship that they shared? The thought made panic bubble underneath his rib cage, drowning out pain and making him want to do something, anything that would at least preserve their friendship. If they had that friendship, maybe they could build something on it at some point in the future, but he couldn't build anything if he didn't have anything to begin with.

"I'm sorry about that. It was...out of line. I shouldn't have done it."

Her head jerked up, and she looked back at him with wide eyes.

Those bright green eyes that he saw so clearly in his dreams, only usually they looked a little happier, maybe with some adoration, and a smile on her lips below them. Now, they held surprise and then irritation.

"I shouldn't have played along. It was a stupid thing to do."

Her words were tossed out, but she was disgusted with herself. Or with him. Most likely with him.

"Sorry. I... You've been so good to me. I value your friendship, and I don't want to do anything that would ruin that. I shouldn't have said anything about that, and I just... I hope you'll forgive me."

Maybe if he felt better, he'd walk over and get down on his knees in front of her and beg her to continue to be friends with him and to forget that he was such an idiot, maybe if he could say words, the words to explain he had a crush on her, had for almost a decade, wanted her to return his feelings, wanted to have a relationship and move forward, get married and have children and grow old together... Yeah. He could tell her all of those things, and then he would really ruin the relationship that they had.

Sometimes he was such an idiot.

"Sondra. Please. What can I do?" He tried to keep the panic out of his voice. He didn't want her to be mad at him and demand that he take her home. He would. He wasn't sure he could make an eight-hour drive right now, but he'd try, if that's what she wanted.

She poked the fire harder than she needed to, one last time, and then she stood up, shutting the door, looking at the pot on the stove.

"Sondra?"

He should just shut up. If she wanted to be mad at him, if she wanted to hate him for the rest of her life, she could. And he deserved it.

"I'd just really like to stay friends," he said, and he hoped his tone was cajoling but not too wimpy. He didn't like wimpy men, and he certainly couldn't expect Sondra to. But at the same time, he would be humble for her, if it would keep their friendship intact.

He had lost hope that there would be anything more, which was hard, after the feelings that he felt with that kiss. It had completely knocked his heart for a loop and been so much more than what he had expected.

"We're still friends, okay? Just don't ask for that again." She threw the words back over her shoulder at him as she walked over to the table, taking the knife and chopping the cream cheese into even smaller pieces.

"It doesn't sound like we are. Sounds like you're mad at me."

"Well, I am. I don't know why you have to be so...frustrating."

At least she was talking to him. Of course, Sondra wasn't exactly the type of person who would be very good at giving anyone the silent treatment. She couldn't keep from talking for more than a few minutes at most. Although usually she was talking about her shows, the Hollywood stuff she loved, but that had faded away the longer they'd been there.

"I'm sorry. I frustrate myself sometimes too." He could agree with that. She was right. He was an idiot. He couldn't build a relationship with someone by demanding that they kiss him as a reward for sitting still. How juvenile was that? It would serve him right if she considered him a kindergarten kisser, considering that what he had just done was definitely elementary school.

Surprisingly, she didn't really say much as she finished cooking supper, and he sat gingerly in a chair. It had been the first time that he'd spent more than an hour out of bed since the accident, and he was shaking with weakness as they finished supper.

He wanted to get up and help her with the dishes. Wanted to help clear off the table and sit outside on the porch, watching the night descend into the woods. It was his favorite time of day, after sunrise.

He could do it. He had enough left in him to help her clear the table, then he would collapse in bed, and maybe even take a pain pill, because his headache had gotten worse.

He started to stand.

"If you're not getting up to go straight to bed, you just stay right there," Sondra said, and her voice did not sound friendly or nice or happy, but it was a direct and deliberate command, like she expected to be obeyed.

"Um, I was going to help you clear up the table," he said, and he hated the breathless way his voice sounded.

"You're out of breath just sitting there. You definitely are not getting up to touch a dish. And if you do, I can take you down right now."

He stared at her for a second, and then he couldn't help it but a little grin lifted the corners of his lips, and he said, "If you think that's a kind of threat, you can't be upset when I deliberately do what you're asking me not to do, just because I want to see the consequences of my actions."

He knew he shouldn't tease her. They weren't in that kind of standing with their relationship. He didn't really have the leeway to try to make her smile and give her a hard time.

But maybe that was a little bit of a smile that tugged at her lips. "It's not going to be pretty. And considering that I'm the one that has to clean up the mess, you'd better tread pretty lightly. Because I might choose not to."

"I'll tell you what, I'll sit here in the chair, if you let me sit out on the porch this evening for a little bit." He hated how weak he felt and that the idea of sitting on the porch made him feel a little dizzy.

"You can sit on the porch, if you go to bed right now and lie down for a bit."

If he did that, he'd fall asleep, unless his headache kept him awake.

But she was right, and he knew it. She could tell that he needed the rest, that he overextended himself and probably would feel worse the next day, rather than better. He wanted to get better. He wanted to push himself.

"And if we're going to drive to town tomorrow, you might want to skip it altogether."

"It feels like there's going to be a storm. I want to watch it."

"A storm?" Her eyes widened, and he berated himself for saying anything. She'd been doing so good, he'd kind of forgotten that staying here wasn't really her thing.

"I could be wrong. It just...feels like it."

"So you can't tell from the wind or from looking outside, it's just something you're feeling?"

"I guess standing out there, it just... There's a smell or something. I just thought there might be a thunderstorm tonight."

"I'm terrified of thunderstorms," she whispered, holding a fork in one hand and a plate in the other. "How bad do you think it's going to be?"

"I don't even know if there's going to be one. I wish I wouldn't have said anything."

"I'm glad you did. I can be prepared."

She moved over and looked at the notebook that she'd been keeping beside her at all times. He noticed that she had copied verses down from the Bible, but he'd given her plenty of privacy and had not tried to look over her shoulder at all, not trying to figure out what she wrote.

Although, when she read aloud to him, which he loved, because her voice was soothing and just...made him feel calm and happy, she almost always read from Psalms.

She had taken it upon herself to tackle the fear that lived inside of her. He had thought more than once that she used TV, her Hollywood people, and her deep interest in those types of things to cover or attempt to soothe the fear and anxiety that lived inside of her.

She hadn't had that here, and she'd filled that with the Psalms. There really wasn't a better book in the Bible to use when a person was afraid. He'd done it himself more than once.

Particularly after his parents had died. That had been a real blow to him. They had seemed so much bigger than life. Like nothing could ever happen to them, and the fact that they had been gone, snatched away so quickly, had been hard to reconcile in his mind. They were never coming back.

The Bible had been such a comfort at that time.

"I'll lie down. But if I fall asleep, and it starts to storm, would you wake me up, please?"

"If you fall asleep, I'm definitely not going to wake you up. I can tell from the pinched look around your eyes and the tightness around your mouth that you're in a lot of pain right now."

He had started to hobble toward the bedroom, but her words made him stop, and he put a hand on the chair for balance as he looked at her. "You can tell all that by looking at me?"

"Sure." She lifted her shoulder and continued to wash the dishes at the sink.

He couldn't believe that she paid that kind of attention to him. Of course, she'd been taking care of him for a week and a half, but more because she was forced to, like she didn't have a choice. He was her ticket out of there, not because she cared. But that was something a person who paid attention because they cared would notice.

He wasn't sure how he knew the difference, he just knew there was a difference.

Regardless, she didn't seem inclined to talk about it, or to talk about anything, which was a switch, and it bothered him. But he wasn't sure what to do about it.

He didn't say anything more to her, because he'd already dug himself into such a deep hole, and he had no idea how to get out. So, he walked into the bedroom and lowered himself carefully on the bed, stretching out in relief. It didn't help with the pain, but his muscles sighed in relief, and before he knew it, he was sleeping.

Chapter Twenty-One

Lightning flashed across the sky. It made Sondra jump up from the step where she sat.

There had been gusts of wind, and the evening was much different than the other evenings where she sat on the porch and watched the night come down.

She thought that Asher was probably right about the storm that was coming, and she held her notebook with both hands. She'd been working on memorizing verses as she sat there until it had gotten too dark.

Now, the lightning showed that Asher's feeling was right.

She didn't think that men had feelings. She'd expected he would base his thought on some kind of scientific data, but instead, he said he just felt like it was. That was so weird.

But she didn't want to think about Asher. Every time she did, her heart cramped up, and her throat closed.

He had apologized for kissing her! He wanted to just be friends. He didn't want to ruin their friendship.

She wanted to spit in his face. How dare he kiss her like that, turn her entire world upside down, and then apologize for it and tell her he just wanted to be friends?

She wanted to grab a hold of his neck and squeeze, except she didn't want to hurt him. Even now, when she was so furiously angry, not really angry at him, angry at herself for being so stupid. She... She was developing deep, strong feelings for him. Definitely way more than friend feelings.

That kiss.

On the outside, anyone watching would have thought it was so simple, as to be almost childish, but from where she stood, it had shifted her entire world. And he apologized.

Said the "friend" word.

She almost told him that she wanted to go home immediately. But one look at him, the pallor underneath his natural tan, the beads of sweat on his forehead, and the pinched look on his face told her he was in deep pain, not to mention, the way his body shook from exhaustion, from just walking out on the porch, all of those were strong indicators that he absolutely could not drive eight hours to get home. Even driving an hour to the grocery store was going to tax him, especially if he couldn't make it down the front stairs without taking a break.

But she needed to get away. She needed to put some distance between them, or she was going to end up totally and completely falling for someone who was absolutely wrong for her. After all, if he apologized after kissing her and told her he wanted to be friends, then there was no hope for the feelings she had.

There hadn't been anything in Psalms about unrequited love and what a person was supposed to do when the man they found themselves falling for didn't want them.

Lightning flashed, and this time, thunder rumbled in the distance, and she jerked to her feet.

Thunderstorms were something she feared more than anything else.

She'd never even seen a tornado, but thunderstorms, with their gusty wind, their powerful lightning, and the hail and wicked rain that went along with them always petrified her. She hated them.

The hair stood up on the back of her neck, and her stomach roiled, worse than the leaves of the trees around her. She eyed them. There were plenty of trees close enough to the cabin that if they blew down would hit it. Hit her.

She turned and hurried into the cabin, shutting the door behind her and leaning against it, panting.

She had made a pallet out of the blankets and rolled it out each night beside the stove. There were a couple of nights she had been chilly, but never anything that had driven her into Asher's room to get warm.

He had told her several times that if she needed to, it was okay. And she hadn't read anything into that invitation other than survival. He trusted her to be wise enough to know that if she was cold, she needed to come in and get warmed up. Sharing body heat just made sense in the conditions that they were in.

But this was something completely different. This was fear, deep and primal and bordering on panic.

She looked wildly around the room. Under the table would be the safest place. But she could just see Asher coming out of the bedroom, squinting in the dark trying to find her, and seeing her shadow under the table, cowering.

No.

It wasn't that cold, but...could she pretend she was cold?

She didn't want to lie. But maybe, she could just shiver a little, and he would assume that she was cold, and he wouldn't realize that she was scared when she slipped into bed with him.

Another streak of lightning lit up the cabin with its blinking brightness, and Sondra held her breath. One, two, three, she made it the whole way to seven before the crack of thunder made her jump and a small exclamation of fear pressed out of her lips.

She set the notebook on the table as she hurried by.

She didn't care what Asher thought, she was climbing into bed with him and holding on tight. If she were home, she would have the TV on, the volume up, and be watching whatever her favorite show was at the time.

If the lights went out and the TV shut off, she would have something else downloaded on her phone to take her attention. There was always a backup. Something, anything that would take her mind off the storm raging outside.

The LORD is good, a strong hold in the day of trouble; and he knoweth them that trust in him.

She took a deep breath. She could do this. God was with her, and he had provided Asher for her to cling to during this difficult time.

She wasn't entirely sure that was true, but she made that rationalization in her head and tried to control herself as she fumbled with the door to get into the bedroom.

Another streak of lightning lit the room up like it was daylight, flashing and blinking as she made her way to the bed.

She didn't know how Asher could sleep through it, but she heard his steady breathing. Of course, he pushed himself further than he had pushed himself since his accident, and he was probably exhausted. She hoped she didn't wake him up. With the way he had been in pain, it had probably been a struggle to get to sleep.

She felt a little bad for the unkind way she had treated him. But how was she supposed to explain that she liked him too much? That his apology, as sweet and kind as it was, that his insistence that he didn't want to ruin their "friendship" had hurt her more than if he'd told her she was a terrible kisser and he never wanted to touch her again.

Why couldn't he have come in and told her that kiss had knocked him through a loop, and he wanted to do something about it. Something more.

Even if he hadn't pledged his undying love to her, just...something more than *man, I shouldn't have kissed you. That was a big mistake.*

He hadn't called it a mistake, but that's what she had heard when he apologized. That he thought what he had done with her was a mistake.

She couldn't say the same, she couldn't say even close to the same.

Another crack of lightning split the room and made her jump as she reached the bed and felt for where Asher lay in it. She didn't want to hurt him, so she made sure she was on his right side, and then she didn't have to pretend to be shivering, although the shivering was because of fear, not cold.

She lifted the covers and carefully got under, trying to hold herself a little bit apart, because she didn't want him to get the wrong idea. This was not supposed to be suggestive in any way, although...she supposed there was a part of her that appreciated the fact that the one person she had to cling to was the person she couldn't stop thinking about, admiring, and being upset with, because he didn't want to have anything to do with her.

It wasn't his fault. She couldn't be mad at him for being honest about his feelings. If he didn't have any feelings for her, she wouldn't want him to pretend that he did, so it was silly for her to get upset about that apology.

Another flash of lightning, and immediately after that, the rain started drumming on the roof, almost deafening in its sound. It must have been some kind of metal roof or something, or maybe it was hail coming down. She wasn't sure. Would it break through the ceiling?

She grabbed a hold of Asher's arm, putting her hands around his bicep and trying not to squeeze hard enough that she cut off his circulation. Her feet found his leg, and she pressed herself as close to him as she could, without draping herself over him.

"Sondra?" he said sleepily, moving a bit and then gasping, she assumed because of the pain.

"Sorry. It's...cold out." She said the words a lot faster than she should have, and she didn't even believe herself. She certainly couldn't expect him to believe her.

"Yeah. I hear how cold it is."

She wanted to laugh, but she also wanted to cry at the same time, and she also wanted to beg him to not make her leave.

"Sorry." Her voice sounded tight and high. "Please don't make me go."

"Never. I would never make you go."

His words still sounded like sleep clung to them, but he woke up faster than she did and seemed cognizant of everything that was going on. There might have been a little bit of humor in his voice, but he shifted some, moving his arm, and she had to pry her fingers up as he took it out of her grasp, keeping herself from grabbing a hold of him, just in time, as she remembered his broken ribs.

"Here. I'm going to put my arm around you."

"I don't want to hurt you." But she didn't want to leave him either. And she did want him closer.

"It's my right side. It's okay."

She lifted her head as his arm moved, and true to his word, it came around her, holding her shoulders close and tugging her to him. If it hurt him, she couldn't tell.

"Put your arm around me. It's okay."

She put it down on his stomach, with her hand on his hip bone, before she slid around, pressing close.

"I'm sorry. I'm petrified of thunderstorms."

"I remember."

He did? She couldn't remember going through a thunderstorm with him, but she had been visiting Ezra once when one had happened.

She remembered now. She embarrassed herself, because she tried to cling to Ezra, and he had launched into an explanation of why they didn't need to be afraid of thunderstorms, and if they were truly frightened of a tornado, they could go down to the basement. That everything would be fine, and that there was no need to be afraid.

He seemed to think his logic would calm her fears and that after she had listened to him lecture her about the science behind thunderstorms, she should be just as calm as he was.

She ended up grabbing their dog, and going into the bathroom, and huddling on the floor by herself, pulling up a video on her phone, and turning the sound up as loud as she could, which did nothing to drown out the sound of the thunder, and the only thing that made her feel even slightly less like a kindergartner was the fact that the dog was just as afraid of the thunderstorm as she was.

That was the day she found a kindred spirit in Houser, their dog, who they had lost shortly after, and she had cried harder than any of the Clybourns, because of their shared time in the bathroom.

She thought maybe she liked that dog better than she liked Ezra.

Chapter Twenty-Two

"You noticed?" Sondra finally said as the rain continued to pound down, heavy at times and then softening, almost as though different bands were going through, but she could hear the winds, whipping and blowing, and there must have been a crack in the wall by the window, because it whistled at times depending on the direction it blew.

"Yeah. I sat outside the bathroom, but...I didn't knock on the door, because, well, because I was the little brother, and I figured that you probably didn't want to see me."

She hadn't even noticed him. She didn't really remember seeing him much at all when she and Ezra were together. He was just...one of the little ones.

"You weren't there when I got out." The thunderstorm had been over for a while, and she watched another show before she and Houser had left the bathroom.

"No. Once the storm was over, I listened until I heard you moving, and I figured you were okay. I didn't really want you to see me out there. But I wanted to be there in case you needed me."

She found Ezra later, sitting on the recliner in the living room, casually reading the Market News livestock report.

"Thank you. Thank you for caring," she finally said. Thinking that she probably shouldn't have stayed with Ezra as long as she did, but she had been in love with the idea of being a part of the Clybourn family.

He didn't say anything, and she figured that maybe he was thinking about how he just wanted to be friends with her, and she had made him uncomfortable by climbing into bed with him. And then thanked him for caring.

She pressed her mouth closed, although she couldn't help squeezing tight the next time lighting struck and lit up the room.

His hand moved gently up and down her arm, and it felt like his lips touched the top of her head. She probably imagined that though, considering that he wanted to stay friends, and that she had made him uncomfortable by thinking that there was going to be more. After all, his apology for the kiss that had blown her away was still fresh in her mind.

Still, comforting each other during a thunderstorm when one was petrified was probably something that friends did for each other.

It made her wonder if Ezra was even her friend. She didn't want to fault Ezra though, because she hadn't wanted to listen to him when he had suggested cooling down the relationship. In fact, she had insisted that they were engaged, when he really didn't want to be.

If she was going to turn over a new leaf, if she was going to change the way she was, she couldn't just assume that the guy that she was interested in wanted the same things she did. She should step back and allow him to...put their relationship in the friend zone if that's what he wanted.

She probably should have done that with Ezra a long time before. But she could be a person who learned from her mistakes.

Thunder rumbled, and then lightning struck so close they could hear the crack and almost feel the electricity in the air.

She jumped and remembered just in time not to squeeze too hard, although her hands grabbed a fistful of his T-shirt and she couldn't stop her body from trembling.

He started to sing, and that was better than any of her shows, having him beside her, right there for her to hold onto, while his voice soothed her soul.

After she listened for a bit, she joined in, remembering the verse that said:

I call to remembrance my song in the night.

The Lord's our Rock, in Him we hide,
A Shelter in the time of storm;
Secure whatever ill betide,
A Shelter in the time of storm.
A shade by day, defense by night,
A Shelter in the time of storm;
No fears alarm, no foes affright,
A Shelter in the time of storm.
The raging storms may round us beat,
A Shelter in the time of storm;
We'll never leave our safe Retreat,
A Shelter in the time of storm.
O Rock divine, O Refuge dear,
A Shelter in the time of storm;
Be Thou our Helper ever near,
A Shelter in the time of storm.
Oh, Jesus is a Rock in a weary land, A weary land, a weary land;
Oh, Jesus is a Rock in a weary land, A Shelter in the time of storm.

As their voices mingled together in harmony, she realized that she really didn't have any fear while they were singing together. God's commands never ceased to amaze her, at how they were always the best thing for them. Maybe He was onto something when He commanded them to sing. Maybe He knew that it would help calm her anxiety and make her panic disappear.

"That really helps. What a great idea."

"I just like listening to you. I figured if I started, you'd start singing too. Maybe I was afraid and needed to listen to your voice in order to not panic."

She laughed a little. The storm seemed to lessen in its intensity, or maybe she just felt a lot more relaxed. She felt warm and safe, and although there was still some bitter disappointment because she knew her feelings were not returned, there was still the confidence and security that a person felt when they knew they were in the presence of a friend. Someone who wanted the best for them and who would do whatever they needed to in order to keep her safe and secure.

Asher might not care for her the way she wanted him to, but she knew he did care.

His words made her laugh though.

"I'm not that great of a singer." She rolled her eyes, although he couldn't see it in the dark.

His hand had started moving up and down her arm, and her own fingers touched over the fabric of his T-shirt, feeling the hardness of his waist and being reassured of the strength that was there, even if he was laid up.

"I'm glad you came in," he finally said. After they lay there, listening to the rain. "I know thunderstorms scare you, but I love them. There's just something about them that makes me feel...energized, I guess."

"It definitely shows you the power of God." She could give that much. And it was nice to know that he didn't resent her for waking him up.

"That too. It's kind of nice to know that He keeps you in the palm of His hand. Someone as strong as what God must be to control all of that is certainly capable of protecting us."

"That's true. I guess I don't think about those kinds of things. I just...get so caught up in how scared I am that I don't really think about anything else."

"I know it's tempting to let yourself sink down in your fear, and it takes time and effort to fight that, the way you've been doing this past week or so. It's been impressive."

"Kind of the way that you fought to get out of bed and walk, even though you're in pain. I hope I didn't wake you up, because I figured it was probably hard for you to get sleep with the way you are hurting today."

"I probably pushed it a little bit too hard, but I ended up taking a pain pill, which knocks the edge off enough that I can sleep."

"How's your head feeling?"

"My headache is mostly gone. I think... I think it's you."

She laughed. "You're just trying to make me feel better and not like a two-year-old who crawled into mommy and daddy's bed during the thunderstorm because they were scared."

"Yeah. I don't want you to feel like that."

He didn't say anything more, and she wasn't exactly sure what he meant by that comment. Maybe he just didn't want her to feel like a two-year-old. Or...she wasn't sure.

"Aren't you ever scared?" she asked, feeling sleepy, knowing that it was time for her to get up and leave, but she didn't want to.

"Sure. I was really afraid when my parents died."

"You were? I don't remember that. I mean, Ezra took it really hard, but you know Ezra, him taking something to heart is just him being quiet for a week."

"Yeah. I don't think he said more than three sentences the whole week after they died. Other than what he had to do in order to organize the funeral and make the burial arrangements."

"I thought that would have been hard, knowing he had to take over everything, and being so shocked and saddened at the death of his parents, and still having to arrange the funeral as well."

"I'm sure it was. He and Phoebe and Priscilla and Caleb took on most of the burden. I just... I felt like I had my whole rock moved, everything I built my world on came crashing down. I suppose that's when I realized that what I thought had been a foundation in Christ was a foundation in my family. And my parents in particular. I suppose I still lean on my family some. It's kind of hard not to when you work with them like I do. But it definitely made me more aware that I need to take stock of my life and make sure that I'm not using something as a crutch, something to keep my fears at bay, something other than God."

"Yeah. Like I was doing with my shows. I... I can see that now. I was anxious and almost in a full-blown state of panic for the first day or so that I was here. I figured out the exact same thing. That I was using that as a crutch. The noise in the background made me feel like I wasn't alone. Instead of looking to God, I looked to Hollywood to make me happy."

"I think sometimes we do that with Christmas too. I know that's something I struggle with. Just the holidays without my parents. It's easy to fill them with a bunch of stuff, but then we lose the real reason of the season, because we want to recreate our memories to make ourselves feel good."

"I guess so. I don't really have any good memories of Christmas."

His arm stopped, and then his hand, warm and rough, gripped her arm, and he squeezed.

"I'm sorry. I can't even imagine growing up as an only child and having parents like yours, who...didn't really care."

"Yeah. They cared. Long enough to take a good family picture and send it to a hundred people. It really didn't do a whole lot for me though."

"Children are the whole reason we have a family. It's not about parents making themselves feel good and impressing all of their friends. It's about the bonds that you have and the memories you make together."

"Yeah. I guess I just don't have any of that. My memories very much include the actors and actresses that I felt like I knew, but...I really don't. I have no idea what's going on in their lives. I don't know anything about them. And I felt like they were friends, but they didn't even know me. Or anything about me. They're certainly not around when I need them. It's so weird. About how I could get caught up in all that. But I realized that I could quote whole scenes of movies and know exactly what was happening in every episode of the show that I've watched three or four times, and yet I knew nothing from the Bible."

"I've seen you sometimes, thinking that you are memorizing, as you close your eyes and your mouth would be moving. Of course, I couldn't figure out whether you were memorizing or praying. They kinda look the same."

"Yeah. I don't usually move my mouth when I'm praying. God hears our thoughts, right?"

"The Bible says he does. ***O LORD, thou hast searched me, and known me. Thou knowest my downsitting and mine uprising, thou understandest my thought afar off.***"

"I didn't know that. Where's that verse?"

"In Psalms."

"That's comforting. Well, there's so much in the Bible that I've been missing."

"Yeah. I guess it was after my parents died that I started reading the Bible seriously. After all, I'd kind of been depending on them to get to heaven. I knew I had made my own profession of faith, but I'd been depending on them to know what was right and wrong, I had never really taken the time to figure out for myself what I actually believed and why I believed it. I mean, I just believed it because that's what people said."

"I do that."

"Yeah. I did too. But do you realize how much people say, even Christians, that doesn't line up with what the Bible tells us? I was shocked and appalled as I went through the Bible, each time I read through it, things jumped out at me that were so completely opposite as to what the world tells us."

"You mean, you read it more than once?"

"It's a big book. There's a lot of information in it. And yeah, every time I read it, I get something new. And a lot of times, those things that I see and understand go completely against what the world tells us. You know one that's really controversial?"

"No. What?"

"The Bible says ***Withhold not correction from the child: for if thou beatest him with the rod, he shall not die. Thou shalt beat him with the rod, and shalt deliver his soul from hell.*** What do you suppose that means? Are we supposed to spank our kids? Here's another one: ***The rod and reproof giveth wisdom.***" He was quiet for a moment. "Do you think the Bible is wrong? I mean, we should spank our children according to that."

"Using a rod," she said.

"Chasten thy son while there is hope, and let not thy soul spare for his crying."

"We're not supposed to not punish our children just because we feel pity for them."

"God punishes us. It's clear in the Bible that He says He does, and sometimes it's a lot more painful than a spanking. I don't think He was joking when He said that parents are to punish their children as well.

Punishment is supposed to be a part of character growth. God uses it for us. Why wouldn't we use it for our kids? But you won't find a single popular Christian teacher who will tell you that. Do we not use the Bible when we're raising our children? Do we as humans think we know better than God?"

"That's a hard teaching."

"Yeah. Very hard. I think a lot of people told Jesus that His teachings were hard as well, and yet, they work."

They fell quiet, but her mind was whirling. He was right. She had no idea that the Bible said that. But...God wrote the Bible. Was He wrong?

Of course, things were a lot more violent back in Bible times, but if God was capable of doing anything, He could have kept that violence out of the Bible if that's what He wanted, but it wasn't. She supposed punishing a child taught them that there were consequences for their actions.

She wanted to argue. She wanted to tell him that he was wrong, but she didn't know enough of the Bible to be able to pick out a verse to say hey, this is what God really wants us to do, and it's not to spank our kids. But maybe she could read the Bible. Maybe she could find that verse. Maybe she could present an argument that would say that she was right.

But if she was wrong, could she accept that? Could she believe that punishment was actually an important and necessary and God-commanded way of child-rearing?

Not that she had any kids, or that she even needed to worry about it.

But Asher had made a great point. He had shocked her, by quoting verses she hadn't even known were in the Bible, and shown her that maybe the things that people said were not always things she should believe. But she should go to the Bible and look for it herself. And not believe someone just because they sounded rational or reasonable or because they said words that she wanted to hear.

She remembered some kind of verse about itching ears. Where people listened to things because they wanted to hear them, and they ignored the things they didn't want to. The Bible warned that would happen. And yet, wasn't she part of that problem?

The rain had tapered off to a steady drumming, and she hadn't even noticed when the thunder and lightning stopped. She felt warm and safe and sleepy. Maybe she'd just close her eyes for a few minutes before she slipped out. That was the last thing she thought before everything went blank.

Chapter Twenty-Three

Asher blinked. Sunlight poured in through his window, but there was something heavy on his arm.

He moved his head a little, having learned a week ago that any sudden movement first thing in the morning would send sharp pain throughout his body, and he'd learned to wake up slowly. At least, his mind might switch from knowing nothing to knowing everything, which was typically the way he woke up, but he had trained his body to wake up slowly.

Thus, when he saw the blonde hair that spread over his arm, everything came flooding back, and he remembered the previous night, the storm, Sondra in his arms, singing together, talking softly, her curled up to him and trusting in him to keep her safe.

Even while he tried to point her to God. He couldn't keep her any more safe than any other person or than she could keep herself, really.

But it made him feel good to know that she looked to him. And maybe in a way, God had provided him to be there to help her with her fear. It was much more mental than physical anyway. That was the nature of fear.

If a person had good mental fortitude, they could be considered courageous, and it really had nothing to do with them physically.

He almost thought that mental ability, and the character to control a person's thoughts, had more to do with their success in life than anything else.

Some people just allowed themselves to float, to do whatever felt good, to quit working as soon as possible, and to turn to entertainment to fill all of their spare hours.

It was a mental thing.

In his opinion anyway, but...maybe there was something to be said for lying around, at least, this morning he could appreciate the fact that he really couldn't get out of bed. And he didn't want to.

He just wanted to lie there and enjoy the fact that Sondra was curled up beside him.

What would it be like to wake up with her every morning?

Except, she hadn't liked him kissing her, not at all. And he needed to stop those thoughts. He had just been thinking about how important mental strength was, and yet, he allowed his brain to enjoy the idea of being with Sondra, even though he knew she didn't want him.

Still, he didn't see the harm in enjoying the position that he was in, at least until she woke up and realized where she was.

He didn't expect her to be angry. She was the one who had crawled into his bed. She was the one who had fallen asleep without leaving.

He hadn't done anything, wasn't touching her inappropriately, although he would probably be stroking her arm with his fingers, if her head hadn't been lying on his shoulder and his entire arm wasn't completely numb.

That didn't even bother him. He would certainly put up with that, and a whole lot more, just to have her beside him.

For as long as she'd let him.

His thoughts turned to today, and the fact that he was going to try to make it down the mountain. He knew the best idea was to go. If he went an entire day without food, tomorrow he wouldn't be any stronger.

But he wasn't entirely sure it was safe for him to drive.

It was going to hurt, no matter what he did, but at least if he was in the passenger seat, he wasn't going to black out and wreck his truck. So he had two options, see if Sondra would drive, while he rode with her, or go by himself and leave her there. He didn't want her to be in the pickup while he was driving, in case he blacked out.

Not to mention, the roads were rural and almost always deserted, but on the off chance that he were to meet a car at the same time he passed out, he wouldn't want to hurt anyone.

Of course, once he got to town, he wasn't sure he had the energy to go through the grocery store and pick up what they needed.

He would almost certainly have to have Sondra with him.

And that meant she would have to drive. He turned his head, his lips brushing her hair, as he breathed in her scent. It was pure, with no artificial soap or shampoo to clog up the smell that was purely and uniquely hers. It smelled completely right to him. Like the smell of petrichor. Or a newborn calf. Puppy breath.

Yeah, definitely Sondra's scent was in his top five favorite scents. Actually, it was sitting at number one, but he couldn't tell anyone that. Especially not Sondra. He didn't want her getting mad at him again.

He held his breath when she stirred. He wasn't ready for her to get up. He wanted to just lie there and enjoy the morning a little bit more. The only thing that would make it better was if there was a canopy above his head that would open up and let the sunshine and fresh air in. That would be pretty much perfect.

But apparently when he made his cabin, he hadn't had the foresight that he had now, and he hadn't done that. So, he waited as she shifted, looking down into her face as her lips twitched, she smiled a little, and then her eyes opened, sleepy and dreamy and looking up at him like he was the hero of whatever dream she had been having.

"Asher. Good morning," she murmured. The smile on her face grew bigger.

Then, to his surprise, she turned her head and pressed her lips against his neck.

His heart stopped, and every cell in his body went on high alert. It was a soft touch but precious, and he closed his eyes. Wishing that she had done it when she was wide-awake and knew exactly what she was doing. Her lips moved, and his fingers curled. He wanted to pull her closer and drop his own lips to her forehead, and maybe she would lift her head, and they would share another kiss, better than the one that they had on the porch.

But he could feel her body when it froze, and she woke fully and remembered where she was and what she was doing and who she was doing it with.

"Oh. I'm sorry," she said, and she sounded a little breathless as she jerked back, then she seemed to remember just in time about his injuries, and her hand, the one that had been resting on his hip bone, stopped in the middle of his stomach where his T-shirt had worked up during the night, and it lay on bare skin.

He wanted to put his hand over top of it, press it close, and not allow her to move it away, but not only would moving his left arm hurt, but she didn't want that anyway. She was only here because she had been afraid of the storm and had fallen asleep.

"Um, I'm sorry. This is a little...awkward. I appreciate you letting me sleep here last night. I didn't mean to stay."

"It was fine. You've been sleeping on the floor. You...should have the bed. In fact, I insist that you take it. I'm well enough that the floor isn't going to hurt me."

"No. As long as you are in pain, you're sleeping in the bed."

He wanted to argue, but he'd already gotten her bossy tone, and he liked the sweet, gentle Sondra better. Although, bossy Sondra was okay too. He kinda liked her as well. She made him smile anyway.

But they had a lot of things that they needed to do or...just one thing. He had to go to town, get groceries, and come back.

"I wanted to go grocery shopping today."

"I don't think you're well enough."

"Well, I think we have two options. The first is I drive to town by myself."

"Why can't I go?" she asked, and a little of the old fear was back in her voice.

There were pinpricks down his arm as she had shifted, and blood was flowing to it again, but he moved his hand up and down her arm anyway.

"I'm afraid that I might black out. I haven't yet. But I don't want to take a chance with you in the seat beside me."

"I would prefer that you not be driving when it happens, either." Her words were a little dry.

He grinned down at her. "Well, that brings us to my second option."

"Which is?" she asked, lifting her brows and tilting her head back so she could see his face.

"You drive."

"By myself?" she asked, her eyes widening and her mouth forming an O.

"I'll sit in the passenger seat, but you would drive. That way, if I can't make it, I'm not going to hurt anyone."

He didn't want to pass out. Didn't even want to consider the possibility, but it was there.

"I don't know if I can drive your truck."

"I figured that. Or else I figured you'd have been asking to drive it before now."

"You figured right." She sighed. "Can I think about it?"

He nodded. Maybe she had to figure out whether or not she was going to be too scared. But one thing he was sure of, he didn't want her to feel like she had no choice.

"If you can't, I know it's just going to be a day or two until I have enough strength that I can without any problems. So, don't feel like you have to, okay? I don't want you to have a panic attack because you think you have to do something you're not sure you can. Although, I wouldn't have suggested it if I thought you couldn't do it."

She nodded. Then she said, "I better get up. Molly is going to wonder where I went."

"Molly?"

"That's what I named the mama raccoon. She's always back in the outhouse well before daylight, but I can hear her churring up there when I go to the bathroom in the morning. She's used to me being out way before this."

"Maybe she had a late night too. I bet she didn't go out until after the storm."

"If she's smart, that's what she did."

They smiled a little bit, and he thought again about how much she changed. From making him stand in front of the door of the outhouse, holding his hands over his ears, to naming the raccoon who lived there and assuming that it missed her in the morning. He shook his head over her whimsy and admitted that maybe he needed something like that in his life.

Chapter Twenty-Four

Sondra gripped the steering wheel tight. It had been a hair-raising experience just to get Asher out to the pickup. She thought he was going to pass out twice, and he was so weak he was shaking. Then, it must have torn him up terribly to climb into the pickup. He needed to use the running board in order to step up and use his right hand to pull himself in with the grab handle.

He was obviously frustrated at his weakness, and that didn't help anything either.

But now, she slowly motored down the dirt road, feeling like she was driving a bus off the side of a mountain.

"How come when you thought of this you were concerned that you might black out and kill me? You never thought that I might have a panic attack and kill you?"

"That wouldn't upset me nearly as much as me harming you."

"Of course not. Because you'd be dead." Her words came out a little snappier than what she meant them to. She was nervous, and petrified, and very, very thankful that she spent so much time memorizing Bible verses. She had been chanting them to herself for the last fifteen minutes.

Asher had told her not to worry about how fast she was going, that she could go as slow as she wanted to. That didn't help. Although, there was a part of her brain that wondered if the brakes would get hot and she would lose them and they would end up going over the mountainside anyway.

She never actually heard of that happening in a pickup, but if it could happen in a big truck, surely pickups were the same?

"Will the brakes get hot?" she asked, trying to lighten her foot up off them, unsuccessfully. She wasn't pressing that hard, because they were only going fifteen miles an hour. How much slower could they go?

"No." His word was said with confidence, even if it was slightly weaker than what his voice usually sounded like. He was obviously in pain, and they had barely even started. At this rate, it was going to take her twice as long as it should, and he would have to spend twice as long out of bed.

She would probably be doing him a favor to speed up.

"Why are you so sure about that?" she asked. "There are runaway ramps for trucks all over the place, where they go if the brakes fail. Don't pickups use those too?"

"No. That's for trucks that are carrying heavy loads. A heavy load will push harder, they'll have to use the brakes more, and that is what causes the brakes to get hot. We don't have any load at all and we're a light pickup, and therefore the amount of force that it's going to take to slow us down is not great enough to cause the brakes to heat."

She thought his explanation sounded reasonable, although she really had no idea. But if he said they were fine, then she supposed she could assume that they were fine.

She had trusted him so far, and he hadn't let her down, although the fact that he was sitting there, in pain and barely able to move, was testament to the fact that he was not perfect.

She wasn't looking for someone who was perfect. After all, she certainly wasn't.

Friends. He wants to be friends.

She hadn't felt the slightest bit friendly toward him this morning when she woke up.

In fact, she felt decidedly more than friendly.

But the kiss that she'd pressed to his neck had made his entire body freeze, and she imagined him struggling not to shove her away. The thought made her sad but had also cleared the rest of the sleep from her mind, and she remembered that she couldn't do such things. Not if she wanted to keep her friend.

After a few more miles of going fifteen miles an hour, she allowed the truck to bump up to twenty. She didn't want to outdrive her abilities and have it going so fast that she couldn't handle something that might come in front of them. Like a turn. A sharp one, of which there were many.

She'd probably gone around six U-turns in the last ten miles.

"What's that?" Asher's voice held warning as he leaned forward, although he winced at the same time. She glanced over and saw his eyes pointed straight ahead, squinting.

She touched the brakes, even as she struggled to process what she saw.

It was a large round shape.

"Is that a bear?" she asked, and her heart leapt into her throat even though she knew there was really no danger. It must've been seventy-five yards off the road, on one of the longer straight stretches.

However, it was just moseying along, across the road, like it didn't have a care in the world. Until it stopped, right in the middle, and turned around and looked back.

She had slowed to a crawl, until they got within fifty yards, and then stopped altogether.

As the bear's head turned toward them, she held her breath. But then, it looked back again, as though expecting something to appear behind it.

"She has cubs," Asher breathed.

Sure enough, Sondra saw a little form hobbling out of the weeds alongside the road and scurrying after its mom. Two more little bundles came after the first one. They were barely up to what she would consider the bear's knees. So cute and small.

"They must be this year's babies. They're tiny."

"Oh my goodness. They're so adorable. Look at them!" she said as they ran into their mom, plopped on their butts, and then started wrestling with each other. It was like they couldn't be serious for even a minute.

Their mom moved her nose over all three of them, as though sniffing to make sure they were all there, before she started moving again.

They sat there and watched until the last form faded off into the woods, and then Sondra looked across the seat, knowing her face was beaming, just because she wanted to share that moment with Asher.

"That was pretty incredible," he said, his own face surely reflecting her emotions.

"I've never seen anything like it." She knew there was wonder in her voice, and rightly so. It was...a thing of nature; she'd lived for more than thirty years and had never seen it herself. "It was amazing."

"Yeah. I... I guess I hope they all make it, although I really don't want to meet them in the cabin clearing anytime soon. Or any time, actually," he said with a small chuckle. Laughing still hurt his ribs, and he winced as he chuckled.

"Yeah. I agree. It's enough to have Molly."

"I'm going to have to go out and see this friend of yours."

"Yeah. If you can make it the whole way to the grocery store, I think you can make it to the outhouse, and I won't have to empty your bedpan anymore."

"You know I owe you for that. That...is a lot more than friendship requires."

"I don't care. I don't mind really. I mean, the first day or two, it was a little bit, you know, icky. But now, I don't even really think about it. It's just something I do, and...I don't mind." And she found that that was true. She didn't mind.

She wished that all of her anxiety had gone away. But she still had moments where it caught up to her. But they were less intense, and she had figured out how to deal with them. Maybe, maybe they would disappear entirely. She hoped so. She believed they would. And she was working toward that end.

There was no further excitement on their way down the mountain, and Sondra caught herself going forty-five miles an hour in a couple of places, once they hit the blacktop and there were actually lines on the road.

That was the last ten miles, and they pulled into the sleepy little town with a single, very small grocery store.

They made a list that morning, and she left Asher in the pickup while she went in and did the shopping.

They had agreed that they would get enough groceries for another week, and then they would assume that he would be strong enough to attempt the eight-hour drive home.

He had said that if he needed to stop after four hours, they could break the drive into two days, and she agreed. She thought that was probably the more likely option, although she hadn't been sure whether he would even make it down the mountain and back up.

In fact, when she came out of the grocery store, she didn't see him in the pickup.

She panicked a little and then tried to calm herself. He was not going to run from her the first second she left him alone for a couple of minutes, and he certainly would take his pickup with him. The fact that his pickup still sat in the parking lot meant that he was somewhere around.

She didn't know why she always had to jump to the worst possible scenario, but it was annoying. Maybe she could work on that too. Going to the best possible scenario rather than the worst. And even if the best didn't work out, at least she would only be disappointed and not petrified, the way she was when she thought about the worst actually happening.

As she pushed the cart by the pickup, she looked in the open passenger window and realized that he had lain down on the seat.

His eyes didn't open as she walked by, and she hoped that he was only resting and hadn't passed out. She wasn't sure what she would do if she wasn't able to wake him up. Could she find her way home on her own?

Surprisingly, the fear that would have elicited last week this time only gave her a passing sense of unease.

She could figure it out. There was plenty of fuel in the truck. He had said he could go another thousand miles almost before stopping to fuel up again. So she could get lost for a really long time before she had to worry about putting fuel in the truck.

By then, hopefully he would be awake and able to direct her.

But then she remembered that he had said that he had wanted to call his family, so she left the cart at the back of the truck, before she emptied any groceries into it, and went back around to wake him up.

He was already shifting and straightening.

"Did you call your family?" she asked, wincing at the tightness around his face and the way his skin held a sheen of perspiration, like dealing with the pain was excruciatingly difficult.

"Yeah. They're fine. They know we're fine. Everything's fine." His voice was kind of a monotone, and he looked exhausted. They'd definitely stressed his abilities further than what they should have pushed.

"I have to empty the cart, and then we'll head home. Would you like a drink?"

"Please," he said.

She went to the back and dug out a bottle of chocolate milk. She had gotten it for that very reason. She figured he'd need a boost and thought that the sugar and the milk would give him the energy he needed to get home. She hoped she figured right.

She had also bought five more packages of cream cheese. She hoped he was around when she emptied the bags of groceries, because she knew that would make him smile.

She smiled to herself as she thought about his reaction and realized that she really wasn't scared. If they had to come back down and get another week's worth of groceries, they would. Sure, she should probably be looking for another job in her business, and she ought to check her emails, but she hadn't even thought about trying to figure out how to charge her phone while they were in civilization.

She found herself...interestingly content. She wouldn't have thought that it was possible, and yet...she was. She wasn't anxious, not much anyway, and she wasn't restless, trying to figure out which TV show she wanted to watch next or longing to know what happened on the last one that she watched that had ended on a cliffhanger, designed to hook people and bring them back for the next episode.

If she had known that purging herself from all social media would make her feel this...good, she would have done it a long time ago.

Again, a little bit of regret for the wasted years, years that she had spent chained to the bondage of Hollywood, made her feel a little down. She'd wasted so much of her life. But she wasn't going to waste any more. Not in regrets, not in servitude to a master who could never be satisfied.

She really needed to thank Asher for opening her eyes and showing her that there was a whole world that she had been missing. Of course, Ezra was part of that too, since if he had honored their engagement, or what she had come to think of as their fake engagement, since it was only her that really believed they were engaged, she wouldn't be here right now. She wouldn't know things that she had learned, and those things had the power to potentially change her life.

Of course, she could see clearly that God had orchestrated it all.

Chapter Twenty-Five

"You know, I think you're going to miss Molly," Asher said quietly as he and Sondra stood and watched the mama raccoon come out with her kits following her.

It had become a ritual that they had done every night since the day after they came home from their second shopping trip.

The first day they'd come home, he'd gone straight to bed and hadn't gotten up until the next morning.

It had completely worn him out, but he also felt like he turned a corner that day too, because from then on, he had been able to get out of bed and walk around the yard every day.

He'd gone to the restroom by himself from then on and had even helped Sondra with the house chores. They cooked together, and like it was in the grocery store, it was fun and casual.

He tried to be the friend she wanted, instead of the potential husband he wanted to be, and she had accepted his friendship overtures just fine.

Once they watched Molly in the evening, they sat on the porch steps until night fell, soft and dark.

She sat a little closer to him than maybe was completely friendly, but he always assumed it was because she was still slightly scared of the night. Although it seemed she had started to really appreciate the things he did.

"Oh, I'm definitely going to miss her. We're going to miss seeing her babies grow up. I mean, how big are they going to be before they stop going home with their mom?" She was quiet for a minute as the last of the babies toddled out of sight. "I guess that would be kinda sad though. You know, they'll just disappear, and we'd never see them again. We won't know what happened to them."

"Yeah. Although, sometimes things are worth the sadness, just enjoying them to begin with."

"True. I wouldn't change this for anything. Even if I knew that they had an unhappy ending. It's been so much fun watching them every evening. And then knowing that they're up there every time I visit the outhouse."

"I might not have noticed if it hadn't been for you." He wouldn't have even been up here if it hadn't been for her. She changed a lot, but he had a lot to thank her for, because she'd taken care of him. "Actually, I wouldn't be alive if it hadn't been for you."

"You know, I thought of that, but you wouldn't have been here, that branch wouldn't have fallen while you were standing underneath it if it hadn't been for me. So you can actually blame me for your accident, even while you're thanking me for making sure you didn't die. You know? It's like a serial killer who changes in the middle and becomes a doctor or something."

"Dr. Jekyll and Mr. Hyde?"

"Maybe a little." She laughed, and he loved the sound.

They turned together, without saying anything, and walked to the steps. As had become their habit, they sat down together, with her sitting close enough that their legs touched.

He knew she didn't really mean anything by it, just...just she still wasn't completely comfortable with the evening.

"I think I'm going to miss this. As shocking as it is to me to say that, I've really fallen in love with your cabin and the woods. Too bad there isn't anything like it close to Sweet Water."

"I love North Dakota, but the mountains definitely give you a taste of something a little different. They're both beautiful examples of God's creation, but vastly different as well."

"I should thank you for teaching me to enjoy it."

"I think you taught yourself. You did a lot of work on yourself while you were up here, and it's pretty amazing what can change in two weeks."

"I have to agree with you there. I hardly ever feel anxiety anymore. I mean, sometimes it's still there, but I know where I can go and what I can do to help me manage it. Where before, I needed Hollywood, and that was not healthy."

"I think a lot of people do that. I wouldn't be too hard on yourself over it. Our whole society is completely addicted to electronics, and if you don't believe me, just look at every hotel room. What's there? The basic necessities and the TV. Same with your vacation homes. There is usually one in every room. And it's fake. Huge. Bigger than the refrigerator, if you can believe that."

"I guess you're right. Our society has...devolved, if that's a word."

"I don't know whether it is or not, but it does feel like we've really gone backward, because instead of being able to relax and entertain ourselves, we depend on someone else to create entertainment for us, and then we just sit and consume it. Although, I guess going even further is the idea that we have so much downtime anyway. Instead of being proactive with our lives, instead of doing constructive things or enjoying God's creation." He chuckled a little. "Like now. We...just seek to do fun stuff. You know, our job is just something we get through until we can go and play."

"It's a little bit embarrassing. It doesn't seem like that's something that adults should do at all, but you're right. It's what our culture does as a whole."

"Everybody's hooked to the internet. And that's a whole world in itself. We get lost in it on a regular basis."

"Yeah. I guess if there's one thing that I've learned the last two weeks, it's that I need to be more mindful of how I spend my time. I don't want to get to the end of my life and realize that I just wasted it on entertainment, and I don't actually have anything of substance to show."

"Or maybe, time spent on family is more important even than productivity."

"I guess you would know about that, since you seem to be the king of family," she said, and she sounded a little sad.

He remembered why he thought she had been after Ezra to begin with, and that was her goal to become part of his family. As much as he wanted Sondra, he didn't want her to be with him just so she could be a part of his family. But maybe there was another way to give her what she wanted, even if it didn't get him what he wanted.

"You know, with your job, you do it online. You can do it anywhere in the world, can't you?"

"I guess so. I need a good internet connection," she said, and she lifted a hand, indicating where they sat. "I couldn't do it here."

"Well, we'd need electricity or some kind of solar setup, that and then satellite internet. But you could do it in Sweet Water."

"Yeah. I guess I could. I'd be closer to your family anyway."

He noticed that she said his family and not necessarily him. Just confirming what he had thought.

"You know, my family could adopt you."

She laughed. "I am almost forty years old. I hardly need to be adopted." She paused for a minute. "I should get married."

"Nah. Not just because you're at a certain age. You have to wait until God brings the right person along. Getting married for the sake of getting married is a really bad idea."

"I know. I suppose that is probably why I'm not married already. Although, maybe that's more because I hadn't been able to find someone who could stand me and want to put up with me for the rest of their life."

"That's a negative way to look at it. I thought you were working on that positive viewpoint."

"It's pretty hard to put a positive spin on that."

"I don't think so. You have a lot to offer someone, and not too many women out there will empty a chamber pot for ten days for a guy who's laid up. I can attest to your vast talent in that area."

"That's awesome. The next time I meet a guy, I'll bring them home and introduce them to you, and you can extol my virtue of chamber pot emptying."

They laughed a little together, and then he said, "I'm serious. The ranch is huge, we can always use help, you know how to cook, as long as you're willing to pitch in, and even if you're not, you could probably find your place and settle down there."

"Don't you think you want to talk to your siblings about that first?"

"Nah. I'm pretty sure they'll go along with it. We've never turned anyone out, you know we've housed a bunch of different people over the years."

"I know. You guys took me in, even when you knew Ezra didn't really like me."

"I didn't know that. Ezra is a hard nut to crack sometimes, although I guess seeing him with Alaska makes me realize that you're right. But I didn't know it at the time."

"I didn't realize either, but that was more because I didn't take the time to listen and try to see."

"Well, that could be." He supposed he agreed with her, but it didn't look very good on her, so he didn't want to be too vocal about it. She did the best she could, and now that she saw a better way, she'd done a really good job of pivoting and trying to turn herself around.

He wanted to tell her that he admired her. That he thought she was amazing. That just sitting here in the dark, with her leg touching his, and her shoulder next to his chest, and her scent on the night breeze, was more than enough for him. But he wanted to be able to be friends with her, even if it never became anything more.

He'd made a move, he had been soundly rebuffed, and he didn't really want to put his heart out there and have it get battered again.

Maybe if they had more time together, because it didn't seem like she hated him. Maybe if he had been well the entire time they'd been there, but God orchestrated it, and maybe this whole time was just so that Sondra could grow, so that she could beat the addiction she had to Hollywood, and conquer her anxiety through God's word. Maybe he was just an accessory to that, and he wasn't meant to be with her.

The thought made him sad and made his heart hurt. He liked her, quite a lot, actually, and the idea that she might be in Sweet Water with him, staying with his family, was so much better than seeing her go back to Wyoming.

"At least consider staying in Sweet Water. With us on the ranch."

"I guess I'll consider it. I would really like to. Your family feels...safe. But maybe I need to go back to Wyoming and be my own person. I guess. Or something."

"You know, God gave us friends for a reason. He didn't expect us to walk through this life with no one else beside us. That's why he gave us a spouse and family, too. You don't happen to have those things, and my family can be that for you. All of that."

"A spouse?" she said, looking over at him from under her brows.

"You never know." He looked back out at the night sky; the stars were shining bright, and the moon had not yet risen. A soft breeze stirred the trees, and the brook murmured soft and low in the inky darkness.

Neither one of them said anything more, and it wasn't much later that they both got up and went to bed for the last time. Planning on leaving bright and early in the morning.

He would look back on these past few weeks as some of the best weeks of his life, despite the pain and hardship, just because they were when he realized what an amazing person Sondra was and his secret crush became a deep love.

<h1 style="text-align:center;font-style:italic">Chapter Twenty-Six</h1>

"This is Asher's favorite kind of chicken. It's not surprising to me that he had to make it while you guys were up there." Claudia grinned at Sondra as she pulled the chicken out of the oven.

"I know. We actually had it twice. He's addicted to the stuff."

The thought of Asher gave her heart a painful squeeze. She had accepted his invitation to stay at the farm for a few days, but she had every intention of returning to Wyoming. It was awkward to see Ezra around and remember how pushy she had been with him. His wife, Alaska, was sweet, as were their two children.

But Sondra needed to move on with her life, and as much as she loved the Clybourns, seeing Asher every day was going to be too painful for her.

Seeing him brought back all her feelings. A deep longing that she knew he would never return. She already cherished the memories of the few weeks they'd spent together. The fun they had, even though it hadn't been easy for her. She had learned more in those few weeks about the Lord, the Bible, and about herself and what she was capable of doing just by changing her thoughts than she ever had before.

She owed most of that to Asher, who had taken her away to begin with. He had done it to save her from herself, she supposed, as well as to help Ezra, and she would always owe him.

She would also always love him. She couldn't imagine feeling the same way about anyone else as she felt about Asher right then. He had been the best thing that had ever happened to her outside of the Lord, and she just couldn't stand being around him every day while he found someone else and fell in love, got married, and had children. No. Just no.

"Agathe is going to love this. It's just the exact right amount for her and her husband." Claudia spoke as though she didn't notice that Sondra had gotten quiet. A couple of the Clybourns had mentioned about her change; it had been obvious to all.

She just hoped she didn't fall back into the same patterns, putting a bandage over the issues that she had, instead of taking them to the Word of God and talking to the Lord about them. That worked so much better.

She and Claudia got in the car and she held the chicken on her lap while they drove to Agathe's place.

Agathe greeted them at the door and invited them in. They went in for a little bit but didn't stay long. Claudia had some errands to run in town, and Sondra was going to pick a few things up too. She intended to head for home the next day.

"Is there anything more that we can do?" Claudia asked as they walked out the door. Her husband had not known who they were, but even more concerning, to Sondra anyway, was that he hadn't known who Agathe was. She said that he would go in and out of times where he knew her and then didn't.

"No. I'm starting the support group next week, and I'm hoping that just having other people around me who are going through the same thing will be helpful. I really appreciate the meal though, sometimes it's just exhausting to...I don't know, be under the stress of knowing that he's leaving me forever. Even though he's still here. It's concerning."

She smiled at them, a benevolent smile that made her look young and beautiful. "Just appreciate the people around you, and don't miss an opportunity to tell them how much you appreciate them and love them. Life is short. Shorter than we realize."

Those words stuck with Sondra as she and Claudia drove into town.

Would she get to the end of her life and regret the fact that she hadn't told Asher how she felt about him? Even though she knew he didn't return her feelings, surely it would be okay for her to tell him how she felt. How she admired him, saw the character that he displayed, and even though she loved him, she could wish him well, wish him health and happiness for the rest of his life.

She didn't really have a hope that he would return her feelings, and she was trying to figure out whether or not it would be beneficial to anyone for her to say anything, when Claudia pulled in to the post office.

"You can come in if you want to. I'm just gonna grab a couple of things that the mail lady couldn't deliver. I'll be right back out."

"You go on in. I... I have a little bit of thinking to do."

"All right. I'll be right back."

Claudia reached for the door handle, and she must not have been paying attention to what she was doing, since she had been looking at Sondra, but Sondra saw the man walking down the street, although she wasn't able to open her mouth to warn Claudia not to open her door too fast.

"Claudia Clybourn! You did that on purpose!" the man snarled. "Can't you see I'm holding a child?"

Sondra thought that Claudia had been on the verge of apologizing when the man snarled at her like that, and...she seemed to recognize him.

"Can't you quit being a jerk? I know it's what you're good at, but why don't you try to grow up for once? I didn't see you, and I really didn't mean to open my door in front of you. But it's not like I touched you or hurt you or anything. Grow up already."

They looked at each other, growling, and if eyes could shoot daggers, they would have been tossing knives around like candy.

The child on the man's hip seemed oblivious and struggled to get down, putting a hand in his beard and grabbing hold of it.

That caused the man to turn his attention to the child, and Sondra was surprised to see how gently he reprimanded the child and extracted the little fingers from his beard.

Interesting. Claudia had been muttering to herself as she got out of the car, seeming to forget about Sondra, slammed the door, and stepped into the post office.

She came out carrying several packages which she put in the back and then got into the front seat. Sondra hadn't figured anything out in her world, but she was curious about Claudia's relationship with the man. So, as soon as Claudia had started on the road back toward the ranch, she said, "Who was that man that you yelled at?"

"Oh, did I yell?" Claudia laughed, and her good humor was completely back. It was weird, like that man had brought out the absolute worst in her. She'd never even seen Claudia angry or upset.

"Yeah. You yelled. And I think you knew him, although I didn't recognize him."

"No. You probably never met him. He's lived in Sweet Water all his life. He thinks he's got all the women in town wrapped around his little fingers, and this chick is not interested."

"I think I got that impression."

"Well, good, because that's the correct impression," Claudia said, and she continued to drive while Sondra thought about the exchange. That man brought out more emotion in Claudia than Sondra had ever seen. She... She thought...Claudia might actually be attracted to him but just acting like she wasn't.

The way Sondra had acted toward Asher.

Sondra wanted to tell Claudia that the man would get the wrong idea if she continued to act angry around him, and then she realized that...maybe Asher had gotten the wrong impression about her.

She tried to think back, trying to remember if there was any indication on his part that he might like her, and she didn't have to think very long.

He had been the one to ask her to kiss him.

Wasn't that indication enough?

And then, the words that Agathe had said came back to her. And she knew that she couldn't go back to Wyoming without telling Asher how she felt. After all, she might have driven him away with the way she acted after their kiss, just because she thought that was what he expected.

She would have to talk to him. Tonight.

<h1 style="text-align: center;">Chapter Twenty-Seven</h1>

"I'm going to see if Sondra wants to stay here."

Asher unhooked the lead from his horse's halter and walked to the fence where Ezra leaned against it, one foot resting on the bottom rung.

"I'd come out to see how you were doing - physically doing. I don't like the fact that you were in such bad shape and didn't ask any of your family for help."

Was Ezra really upset about that? Asher hadn't considered he might be offended. Maybe it was just the idea that he'd worried about Asher.

"I'm sorry. I was in good hands with Sondra."

"I see. Still, that's what your family is for."

"Did you not hear me? I want Sondra to stay here. She's like family."

Ezra's face didn't change other than a slight downturn to one side of his lip. "I heard. And I feel the same. She's like a sister to me."

"So it won't bother you if she stays?" Asking outright was the best policy. Ezra would give him a straight answer, too. He could count on it.

"No. Why would it?" Ezra's face scrunched up. Now was one of those times he wondered if his brother was part robot.

"Because you were engaged to her?"

"I didn't really intend for that to happen."

"What about Alaska? I don't want her to be uncomfortable." If Sondra would ever have him, he wanted to live on the Sweet View Ranch with his family, but if it was going to make his sister-in-law uncomfortable, then he would leave - with Sondra. He didn't want to upset Alaska, but he also would give up his family if it meant he'd get to be with the woman he loved.

"She knows how I felt and how I feel. She's fine. Plus, she likes Sondra."

Ezra sounded like he wasn't quite sure how that happened. "Actually, everyone likes Sondra. She spent so much time with us over the years, she really is like part of the family. And I had a couple of ideas for her."

"You do?"

"Yeah. She's all about social media and all that stuff. She could use her skills and interest to promote the ranch. If she wants, of course."

Asher couldn't believe he hadn't thought of that. "With her design skills, she'd be perfect for that role. I'll have to say something to her."

Ezra nodded, lifting his eyes and squinting at the sun which had dropped low on the horizon. "She's not like a sister to you."

"No."

"When are you going to do something about it?"

"I don't know." He ran a hand over his hair before settling his hat back down on his head. The breeze had died down, and this still time of evening was one of his favorites on the ranch. "I tried to talk to her once, and she didn't seem interested. I thought if I could spend some time with her on the ranch, maybe she'd see me as more than an annoying kid brother."

"I think she already sees you that way."

"I told you, she wasn't interested."

"Are you sure? How long ago was it?"

"Not that long ago."

"Maybe you misunderstood."

"Maybe." He didn't, but he wasn't going to argue with his oldest brother.

"Alaska said you two would be married in three months. She said she thought Sondra had fallen hard for you while you two were at the cabin together."

"You can tell her it was the other way around." Although he'd already been half in love with her before they'd ever made it to the cabin.

"I think you can assume my wife knows what she's talking about. Plus, what do you have to lose?"

"It will be embarrassing if she isn't interested."

"So what? We take risks, embarrass ourselves, get back up, dust ourselves off and keep going. That's life. You can't allow fear to hold you back."

He hadn't considered it was fear. But Ezra was right. He was afraid he'd be embarrassed when Sondra shut him down again. That was keeping him from telling her how he felt. When he thought about how Sondra had fought through her fear and learned to love being at the cabin, fought her fear of driving and took him down the mountain in his truck, fought her fear of the raccoon and even learned to love and appreciate their neighbors...how could he not face his own fear? Now that he knew what was holding him back.

"Maybe the first thing I'll do is see if she'll stay long term."

"You know she's welcome. Mom and Dad never turned anyone who needed a place to stay away. And I can't think of anyone who needs a family more than Sondra."

The sound of a car motor carried to them on the still evening air before they saw the vehicle pulling into the drive.

"Looks like she's back. You won't know unless you say something."

The horses shuffled behind him, one snorted and pawed the ground. The rich equine aroma filled the air. This was what he loved - the ranch, the work, the outside and all the animals and people who made up his home. Would Sondra be happy with him? Could he learn to enjoy the things she did? Or were they too different? Should he back off and allow her to find someone who was more compatible?

"I'm heading in. What you do is up to you. Just know I'll support you, especially if you think the Lord brought you and Sondra together for a reason." Ezra's hand clamped on his shoulder, more like a father than a brother. Ezra had been both to him.

"Thanks."

Ezra nodded, and headed around the larger house to the smaller home where Alaska and their children and he called home.

He was gone before the car stopped in front of the house.

Asher could decide that he would stand back and allow Sondra to find someone who was more compatible, or he could tell her what he wanted and allow her to choose for herself. Put like that, the answer was obvious. Sondra wasn't a child. She was a woman who knew her own mind.

Ezra was right. What did he have to lose? As long as he didn't mind being embarrassed, he had so much more to gain than lose. He grabbed the fence and vaulted over, striding toward the car as Sondra opened her door and stepped out.

"Can I talk to you for a minute?" he asked, before he could chicken out.

"Actually, I was planning on looking you up as soon as I got back, so perfect timing." Her smile could light up his life. Her eyes sparkled and he found himself staring into her face, losing himself in the rush of feelings that came whenever he got close to her. He wanted to blame it on the kiss that wasn't really a kiss at all. Not like he wanted it to be, but that wasn't it and he knew it.

He did want a do-over on that kiss, or another chance, but, more than that, he just wanted to be with Sondra.

"Here I am," he said, trying to shake himself out of whatever spell she seemed to cast on him.

"How are you feeling?" she asked, her brows going down.

"Better. Much better." It probably didn't seem like it, since he was acting a little odd. She must think it was because of his injury. "Walk with me?"

"Sure." Her smile returned and she stepped to his side, turning with him as he moved to go toward the barn. They could walk out along the horse pasture. "Horses aren't raccoons, but there are some foals on the ground."

Her laughter floated on the air. "I did love Molly and her babies, but I'm not looking to replace her. Horses are better for sure."

Her hand swung at her side, and it brushed his once before his fingers tangled with hers. They'd held hands at the cabin many times, but it just seemed...different now that they were home.

"Have you given any thought to staying here?" That wasn't what he wanted to ask. But it was a start, anyway.

"I'd love to. Your family feels more like family to me than my own family does. What there is of it." She ran her thumb over the back of his hand. At least he thought she did. The touch was so light he could barely feel it. "But I don't want to overstay my welcome."

"I was just talking to Ezra about you. He said Alaska likes you and would love for you to stay." He swallowed. Why was this so hard? "So would I."

"Oh?"

She didn't comment on that and he tried to brush off his disappointment. He hadn't declared his undying love or anything.

"Yeah. I...I've gotten used to having you around." Ugh. That was terrible.

"I see."

They had walked past the barn and now strode along the pasture fence, a few curious foals walking on spindly legs, their heads up, sniffing the air like they'd never seen a human before.

"That's not what I wanted to say."

"Okay?" She looked up at him, questions on her face.

He stopped, tugging on her hand so she faced him. He needed to say something that showed her that she was special. Special in a wonderful way...special to him. That he wanted her, not as a sister.

"Are you feeling okay, Asher?" Her voice held concern. "Maybe you've tried to do too much, too fast."

"I'm fine. Physically."

"You have some kind of emotional trauma from your accident?" she asked immediately.

"No." Man, he was really messing this up.

They stood in silence for a few moments, his heart hammering so hard in his chest, it sounded like a wild horse galloping across the prairie.

"Sondra, I love you. I...I've loved you for a long time. But you were with Ezra and I couldn't say anything. I don't expect you to love me now, but I was hoping that if we could spend-"

"I love you, too!"

She interrupted him, and it took him a minute to understand.

"No. I mean, I love you, not like a sister. Like I want to kiss you, marry you...that kind of love."

"Asher. I don't typically go around holding hands with men I only love as a brother. And I've happened to notice that you don't hold your sisters' hands anytime you take a walk with them. In fact, I'm not sure I've seen you ever taking a walk with them."

"You're telling me I'm being an idiot?" He already knew it, but her words made him realize that he might have been being just a little bit blind.

"No. I'm telling you I love you." She stepped a little closer and grinned up at him. "I thought I heard you say the same thing to me."

"I did. I love you. I have for a while."

The smile slipped from her face and a thoughtful look took its place. "Is that why you took me to your cabin?"

Oh. He hadn't thought he'd have to confess that, but it was true. He couldn't deny it. His stomach folded over, but he opened his mouth anyway. "I saw the opportunity to do my brother a favor, I guess. But the main reason is because I wanted to be with you, and couldn't pass that up."

"Really?"

"Yeah."

Her lips turned up and she shook her head. "You wanted me?"

"Yeah. I know I'm not much to look at -"

"You're the perfect leading man." Her hand came up and cupped his cheek. "You kept me safe in the thunderstorm, for one, but more than that, you noticed that they scared me to begin with."

"How could I miss it?"

"You didn't miss it because you cared."

It was true. He did care. "I can't deny it."

"And that makes my heart flutter. That you care about me, that you notice me, that you take the time to do something about what you notice."

"I think she's saying...I'm romantic."

"So romantic." She smiled and lifted her head. "Now, about that kiss we had. I feel like maybe we should practice."

"I guess it did seem like I needed practice. It wasn't that great." Figures he finally got the woman he wanted and he'd left that terrible impression with his kindergarten kissing skills.

"It was the best kiss I ever had." Her expression was sincere.

"It was?"

"It was sweet and gentle and I felt like you cared about me and respected me." She paused. "I've dreamed about that kiss."

His breath caught.

"Me too." Every night.

"As much as I loved that kiss, I hoped we could...maybe try a few different techniques."

"Like you've seen in the movies?"

"No. I think we should create our own movie."

"I'm not sure I want a video camera following us around everywhere."

"No. No camera. A movie just for us." She slipped her hand behind his neck and tugged. She didn't have to ask twice. He lowered his head and spent a good while practicing kissing the woman he loved.

<h1 style="text-align:center">Epilogue</h1>

Claudia stood at the window of the farmhouse, smiling at the couple outlined by the setting sun, as they spoke, then Asher lowered his head. His cowboy hat hid her view of their kiss, but it made her smile, all the same.

The sounds of her family in the living room, her brothers laughing and joking, Alaska's kids squealing and her sisters chattering filled her ears. She pulled her eyes away from Asher.

Nothing made her happier than having her family around and having them happy, seeing their dreams come true.

She folded the tea towel in her hands and hung it over the back of the oven. As things got busier on the ranch, as her siblings got married and started families of their own, her life would change, so she wanted to enjoy these days when everyone was still together as long as she could.

Someday she'd be alone. At least that's the way it felt. Like she was too busy taking care of everyone else to even think about looking around to see if there were any eligible men in Sweet Water.

There was one.

But Beau Hanson was much closer to being her arch enemy than an "eligible" man who might be considered as a marriage prospect. He was much more likely to run over her with his truck than to take her for a ride in it. And that's just the way she wanted it.

At least she tried to tell herself that. Truly she harbored no tender feelings for the guy, even if he was as handsome as sin, and the rest of the town seemed to think he was a man of character and integrity.

He probably was, too. She wasn't quite sure why they'd gotten off on the wrong foot, other than her running into him and knocking him down the first time they met, but that was a huge accident. Maybe he didn't believe her when she explained she hadn't seen him.

Regardless, every time they saw each other, they seemed to push the exact wrong buttons that caused the other one to act in a way that the rest of the town couldn't believe. And Sweet Water as a whole had accepted that they would never be able to stay in each other's presence more than a few minutes, tops.

Plus, Beau lived a quiet life on his family's ranch, which he planned to take over from his dad. He wouldn't be interested in moving onto the Sweet View Ranch, and Claudia wasn't interested in moving away from her family.

It was just as well that they were enemies. Although, truth be told, she wouldn't mind being friends. Maybe she'd just keep that to herself. She wouldn't want him to get the upper hand the next time they met in town. She kind of enjoyed pitting her wits against his and besting him.

With a decisive nod, she moved through the deserted kitchen to join her family in the living room. Family meant everything to her and she would never, ever leave Sweet View Ranch.

Join Jessie's list and be the first to know about new releases and sales on her books!

Read the next book from Sweet View Ranch, *A Cowboy's Heart of Gold*. Could Claudia Clyborne and Beau Hanson use the things life throws at them to look past their differences and forge a strong, forever relationship? And if they do, will one of them have to give up their lifetime dream?

Her piglets were out.

Claudia Clybourn blinked in disbelief from the driver's seat of the old farm truck she had been driving down the main street of Sweet Water, North Dakota.

How had that happened?

Maybe they weren't her piglets. But a glance in the side mirror confirmed that the endgate of her trailer swung wide open.

Great. How was she going to round them up?

"I guess we're going to be chasing piglets for a little bit," she said, trying to keep the frustration out of her voice as she looked over her dog, Ginger, who lay on the seat, and spoke to Mina, the young girl who was staying with her for the summer.

Claudia's friend, Olivia, from when she lived in Wyoming, was going through a hard time with her husband, and her mother had just been diagnosed with cancer. Olivia had been beside herself, trying to figure out how she was going to handle everything and also take care of her daughter who had just gotten out of school for summer break.

The last time Claudia had talked to her, Claudia had volunteered to let Mina come to the Sweet View Ranch for the summer.

Mina had been excited, and Olivia had jumped on the opportunity to send her daughter to someone she trusted and knew would take good care of her.

Olivia had just dropped Mina off the day before, and Claudia and Mina's first outing together was today to pick up piglets and bring them back to the Sweet View Ranch. They would make a great addition to their dude ranch for the summer, plus they'd be food for the winter.

Not that Claudia liked thinking that way, but it was a fact of life on the ranch.

Anyway, it was an inauspicious start.

"Awesome!" Mina said, jerking on her door handle and hopping out. At least Claudia couldn't complain that the girl wasn't eager to help.

She actually really liked Mina. She was a sweet girl and had a great attitude. Olivia had done a good job with her, although Claudia supposed that Mina had some things she was hiding. Nothing serious, just...her parents were going through a difficult time, which was always hard on children. So far, Mina hadn't said anything about it, but in Claudia's experience, kids processed those things deeply, and they came out at the oddest times.

Yanking on the old latch that stuck more than it didn't, she jumped out of the truck, waiting for Ginger, who moved rather slowly in her old age, to clamber out behind her.

Someday soon, Ginger wasn't going to wake up. Claudia didn't want to think about it, since Ginger had been a part of her life for more than half of it. She had ancestors who were herding animals, but her pedigree was so mixed, it was difficult to tell what breed she was.

She was at least eighteen years old and rarely did anything anymore besides walk outside to use the restroom twice a day. But she loved car rides, and when she had seen Claudia leaving this morning with Mina, her sad old eyes had begged Claudia to take her with her, and Claudia couldn't say no to the dog who had been her best friend in the world for so long.

Now, as she waited for Ginger to make her way out of the truck, she tried to figure out how in the world she was going to round up eight piglets. They seemed to be running all over the place.

"I guess we'll just try to sneak up on them and grab them," she said to Mina who had come around the truck and waited for instructions.

"All right." Mina started out, then she stopped and turned around. She was skinny, a typical twelve-year-old who hadn't started to fill out, all legs and arms and elbows and knees, with a big smile that shone with all the metal in her mouth. Olivia had warned Claudia when she dropped her off that Mina would need to go for several orthodontist appointments over the summer.

That meant a long, eight-hour drive back to Wyoming, but Claudia wouldn't mind. If her friend needed help, she would do her best. Of course, they were busy on the ranch, and Claudia was trying to start an orchestra in Sweet Water. Maybe not an orchestra, she would be happy with just a chamber ensemble, but she hadn't realized how expensive sheet music was, and she had spent a lot of long evenings applying for funding.

"What do I do when I catch them?" Mina asked, looking a little confused.

"I guess we'll throw them back in the trailer." Claudia didn't have any better ideas than that. Unfortunately.

Piglets were not exactly her area of expertise.

They hadn't had many of them over the years, because her dad hadn't liked them. He said they were impossible to keep in, they stunk, and the manure wasn't good for anything. And considering all of their downsides, he'd just as soon buy his bacon at the store.

But her parents had died in a car accident a decade ago, leaving her and her eleven siblings to first run the ranch in Wyoming and then the ranch they'd bought here in North Dakota.

There wasn't a day that went by that Claudia didn't miss her parents.

Ginger stood at her heels, and even though she was old and her joints were stiff and she barely did more than walk, she seemed eager at the idea of herding anything. It was an instinct that had been bred into her, and one she'd always taken great delight in using, whether it was cows, horses, pigs, or when they were little, Ginger had herded Claudia's younger siblings quite often.

Claudia remembered her mom getting rather frustrated at the dog who couldn't seem to tell the difference between an animal and a human. Although, they could let the kids out in the yard and didn't have to worry about anyone leaving, because if they tried, Ginger would herd them back in.

And with twelve children, Claudia figured that was actually a help rather than a hindrance. Although her mom had never said.

"There's one!" Mina said, zipping off after the piglet, her long, skinny legs churning. She had turned twelve in the spring but could easily pass for an eight-year-old.

As Mina took off after that one, Claudia saw another one scooting out from underneath a blue sedan. A sedan that looked an awful lot like Reverend Lewis's, pastor of the Sweet Water Methodist Church.

He wasn't exactly known for his patience, but he was known for caring a lot about his car.

Claudia tried to speed walk stealthily, which seemed like a contradiction of terms, toward the piglet.

Ginger walked stiffly at her side.

At least the streets of Sweet Water were deserted, she thought as she managed to get within two feet of the piglet before it saw her and took off in the opposite direction.

She felt like they were never going to get the piglets rounded up, but at least no one was going to witness her folly.

She thought too soon, as a dark green pickup, with tinted windows and familiar custom pipes, pulled into the end of town.

No. It was a rather distinctive truck, and Claudia wanted to drop through the pavement. No. Of all the people who could drive into Sweet Water at this time of day, it could not be Beau Hansen.

She hurried around the edge of Rev. Lewis's teal blue sedan, scrunching down and hoping that a piglet would run out in front of her, so in case anyone—Beau—saw her, it would look like she was actually doing something to help round the piglets up instead of hiding from Beau Hansen. But she was definitely hiding from Beau Hansen.

Except, Ginger didn't follow her. Ginger stayed at the back of the car and let out two loud barks. Almost as though she was telling Claudia that she was going the wrong way and she needed to turn around and get with the program. Ginger of course would be confused as to why

Claudia would be crouching down behind the car instead of chasing the piglets, which was so much more fun.

Even in her advanced age, it was obvious Ginger was eager to round up anything.

"Just give me a minute, okay, Ginger?"

Even to her dog, she didn't want to admit that she was hiding. But it seemed like every time she saw Beau Hansen, he had something unkind to say to her. They had butted heads since her family had first set foot in Sweet Water, eight years ago.

Sometimes in a person's life, there were people that they never got along with, and Beau was that person to Claudia. Odd, because Claudia didn't have a problem getting along with anyone else. As for Beau, she didn't really know. Although part of her wanted to say that he was a jerk to everyone, but she was pretty sure he was well respected in town, and she was the only one who couldn't get along with him.

But every time they bumped into each other, they traded insults, if not butted heads, literally. Since she had run into him and knocked him down the first or second time they met. It was a total accident, because she'd been carrying several large boxes of books she had intended to donate to Sweet Water's used bookstore and coffee shop, except she'd gone in the wrong door.

Understandable, since she couldn't really see anything around the boxes and wasn't familiar with Sweet Water, so as she came out of the grocery store, frustrated with herself because she'd gone in the wrong building, she'd been going a little too fast, hadn't been able to see where she was going, and ran straight into Beau, knocking him on his butt.

She hadn't laughed at the time, although she spent a good bit of time since smiling at the memory of him on the pavement, shock on his face as he looked up at her.

He seemed totally flabbergasted that anyone would dare step into his way, let alone touch him and knock him down.

He was arrogant and egotistical, and that was exactly the kind of thing Claudia could picture him thinking.

But she had been focused on balancing the boxes and laughed a little as the top one jiggled and then settled back down.

He assumed she was laughing at him and had said something

sarcastic. Which she had taken the complete wrong way, because she had been about to ask him if he was okay and offer to set the boxes down so she could help him up.

Anyway, the first meeting had gone rather poorly, and it was all her fault. But she never apologized, because any time she saw him after that, he was so busy insulting her, so by the time she was able to get her mouth open, she found herself insulting him back.

"Just be quiet. Please?" she hissed back at Ginger, not wanting Ginger to draw attention to her. Ginger was well-known around town, since Claudia seldom went to town without her. She wouldn't put it past Beau to see her dog, stop his pickup, and go looking for her, just so he could throw some insults at her and give himself something to smile about for the rest of the day.

He was so annoying.

"I got one!" Mina called from the front of the farm truck.

Squealing noises emphasized that she actually did have a hold on a hog.

"Come help me, please! I can't open the door and hold onto it at the same time. It wiggles too much!"

From through the windows of the car, she could see Beau's pickup was almost beside her. This just seemed to be the way her life seemed to turn out. Of course, she'd have to stand up from beside the car and walk in full view of Beau to the trailer, where she needed to open it.

It stunk, but short of leaving Mina high and dry, she didn't have a choice.

"I'm coming!"

"Is there one underneath the car?" Mina called out. Her voice sounded like she was struggling a bit with the piglet she held. They weren't that big, only about twenty pounds each, but still, twenty pounds of snout and legs and frightened wiggle was enough to keep anyone on their toes.

"Hurry up! I almost dropped it!"

Claudia stood up, careful not to look at the pickup which had slowed to almost a stop right beside Rev. Lewis's distinctive teal car. She could only hope that Beau had slowed because he was looking for a color change for his truck and not because he had seen her crouching down, hiding from him.

She hurried to the back of the trailer, where she pulled the endgate open so Mina could deposit her wiggling and squealing captive inside.

CHAPTER 2

Ginger had followed Claudia but stood just behind Rev. Lewis's car, looking at the pickup and wagging her tail slowly.

Her dog even acted friendly toward that man. Claudia wanted to disown her.

Not really. She loved Ginger way too much to disown her, but part of her love for Ginger was because of Ginger's loyalty.

"Ginger, he is not our friend," she muttered under her breath, just as the pickup shut off, right in the middle of the street, and the tinted window wound down, exposing a face that was way too handsome for its own good.

She wanted to be a good example for Mina, and she could tell that Mina was looking at her, so while she wanted to turn and walk in the opposite direction, she really couldn't.

Except, just then, a pig came squealing out from underneath the trailer, and both she and Mina turned and ran for it at the same time.

Mina lunged just as Claudia bent down to scoop it up. Claudia didn't want to run into Mina, so she swerved but didn't quite lift her foot high enough to get on the curb, and she ended up falling on her side on the hard cement sidewalk.

At least she hadn't fallen just a foot beside her, where there was a picnic bench and a streetlight. She would have hit her head or something. Not that the concrete was a soft landing, because she was pretty sure she had scraped her elbow. Funny how pain didn't really register when her sole purpose in life was getting away from Beau Hansen.

She scrambled to her feet, seeing that Mina had actually caught the pig and was holding it as it wiggled and squealed and tried as hard as its little body could to get away.

"I need the trailer open!" Mina said triumphantly. "I caught another one!" She grinned. "Two for me."

"Yeah. You're doing a great job," Claudia said, realizing that she had hit her hip in a weird way as well, and it hurt as she got up. She tried hard not to limp as she heard soft male laughter behind her.

Grrr. She wanted to wipe the smirk right off his face and shove his laughter back down his throat, but Mina was watching, and she needed to be a good example. So, no physical violence. Although, she allowed herself a few insults in thought only.

And immediately, she felt bad. It was hypocritical for her to put on a good show for Mina and yet allow her thoughts to be mean and unkind. It was no less of a sin, and she said a soft prayer of remorse.

Her thought life was her downfall. She could be kind on the outside, but her thoughts were often the opposite of what she actually acted.

She'd been struggling to get a hold of that for years, and it seemed like she had made no progress.

Still, acting kind, even if she didn't think kind thoughts, was better than being unkind all the way around.

She was only trying to justify her sin, and she knew that.

"Thank you," Mina said in a voice that sounded way too perky and happy for Claudia's mood. "Two down, six more to go! I'll call for you when I need you to open the endgate again."

Mina went running off to find another piglet.

She went up the street, and Claudia figured she should go the opposite direction, but she didn't want to, because that would mean turning around and coming almost face-to-face with Beau Hansen as he sat there in his pickup, probably staring and laughing.

So she turned and stepped up on the sidewalk.

"Good to see you actually can manage to take three steps without running into someone or falling down."

Why did such a nasty person have to have such an amazing voice? It was the kind of voice that made shivers run up and down her backbone. Even when he was insulting her.

She really, really hated it. Truly she did, except...she loved it too.

Deciding that if she ignored bullies they usually went away, she tried to pretend that she didn't hear a thing. And kept walking.

She took three steps before the voice came again, and it was just by her ear. "You're bleeding."

"I have six piglets running around town, and I need to catch them as soon as I can."

"You know, pigs will eat a human, if they think they can get away with it. That blood is going to make them go nuts and probably consume you in some kind of pack violence."

"They're twenty-pound piglets. I'm pretty sure I can handle them. Don't you have somewhere you have to be?"

She kept walking, not even bothering to look to see if there were any piglets around or try to figure out where she should be going. She just wanted to get away from Beau.

"Pigs are filthy. That could get infected."

"And I will take care of it, as soon as I round up the other six pigs."

"Do you need some help?"

"Not from you!" She crossed her arms over her chest and turned to him, planting her feet and opening her mouth. "I heard you laughing. I'm pretty sure if you helped me, all you would do is chase them away from me just so you could sit there and have some kinda sick amusement for your day. Thank you. Just...leave."

Movement caught her eye, and she glanced around Beau, whose wide shoulders seemed to go on forever and ever, to see that one of her piglets had just chased another one of her piglets underneath his truck.

Great. That was exactly what she wanted to have happen. Not.

Without saying anything more to him, she reversed direction and brushed past, trying not to look as foolish as she felt as she power walked and crouched-snuck at the same time to where she could bend down and look underneath his truck.

"Are you trying to disable it so I'll be stuck in the middle of the street for the rest of the day?" he said, and it sounded like he was standing right behind her.

"No. I have two piglets under there. I'm going to try to get them." Then, since he really couldn't leave as long as her pigs were under his truck, she said, "If you want to make yourself helpful, go over to the other side and grab them when they come out."

She didn't expect him to actually do what she told him to. She was just trying to get him to shut up so she could concentrate. It was bad enough that she had to work in front of him. How was she supposed to concentrate when she knew he was making fun of her every move?

She just had to put him out of her mind, except putting Beau out of her mind when he was right there was next to impossible. She might as well pull out her wings and start flying around to catch the piglets.

So, it surprised her when she heard his footsteps move behind her, his cowboy boots making a clumping sound on the pavement as he walked around his truck.

It was a good thing Sweet Water was a small town, although there was typically truck traffic at different times of the day, since the Calhouns had a trucking company at one end of town and Baldwin's sale barn sat at the other end.

Regardless, God definitely blessed them with a quiet moment to grab their runaways, since there hadn't been a single car...except for Beau's.

She wasn't even sure he counted. She didn't want to count him anyway.

But still, it seemed like he was helping her, although she wouldn't put it past him to scare the pigs the whole way to Rockerton.

She didn't really trust him, but she had to let it go, because it needed to be done.

Bending down, she could see both piglets standing nose to nose underneath the truck.

"I'm over here, if you're going to scare them out."

That voice. Ugh. Why did it have to be Beau's voice that had that effect on her backbone? Why couldn't it be someone nice?

Regardless, she said, "Okay. I'm going to see what I can do." She scrunched down, unsure whether to be thankful that his truck did not sit low to the ground, or whether that was a curse, because she had enough room to roll underneath it.

When waving her hands at the piglets didn't work, she stretched out and managed to get her body under the running board and roll to her back.

She flapped her hand at the piglets, unable to roll again but hoping that they would think she was scary enough to take off out the other side.

Sure enough, her movements scared them, and they trotted out, right underneath Beau's stomach. He had crouched down on one knee and had been looking under the truck.

His laughter rang out at the same time the piglets started truly running.

"You missed them!" she said, frustration leaking out of her voice. She had slid the whole way underneath his truck, sacrificing her dignity, to get the piglets picked up, and all he could do was sit there and laugh at her?

She had accomplished her objective, and he had totally messed up.

"Sorry. You should have warned me that it was going to be humorous. After all, it's not every day that I get to see the dignified Claudia Clybourn sliding under my truck."

Dignified? It seemed like all she did when she was around him was land on her face.

"I got another one! I need the back open! Fast!" Mina called, which prompted Claudia to start struggling back out from under his truck.

She didn't bother to look to see if he was still kneeling down and laughing at her or not. She didn't care. At least that's what she told herself. She just needed to get the piglets.

She was so grateful that Mina had managed to get four.

There were only five more running around, although there would only be three if Beau had caught the ones that had just run underneath him, close enough for him to fall on top of.

By the time she had struggled out from under his truck, Beau was already opening the back of the trailer. Mina deposited her piglet inside and looked up at him with shining and happy eyes.

"Thanks! This is fun!" she said, trotting off back toward the front of the farm truck where she came from. "I saw another one up here. I'm going to grab it!" she called over her shoulder as she trotted away.

"Well, looks like the kid is doing better than you are. Whose kid is it anyway?" He paused. "Yours?"

"Yeah. She's mine," Claudia said, and she meant it to come out sarcastically, but she could tell she didn't succeed when Beau said, "I didn't know you had a kid."

She shrugged, not wanting to talk to him more than she needed to. "I also have piglets to pick up. Excuse me."

She felt bad, like maybe he had been holding out a bit of an olive branch, and she had brushed by it. But she was still annoyed that he had laughed at her, twice, plus her arm hurt from where she fell, her hip was burning, and she just crawled underneath his truck for no reason. "Maybe you'll want to get your truck out of the middle of the road," she muttered as she stomped away, trying to figure out where the two piglets that had been under his truck had gone.

"After I help you catch these piglets, I'll do just that. How'd they get loose anyway?"

"I don't know." She must not have latched the endgate tight when she picked them up at the pig farm on the other side of Rockerton. Although, she'd driven for an hour without it coming open, so maybe it had worked its way loose. Maybe she just hadn't shut it quite enough. She didn't typically haul things in the trailer, but eight twenty-pound piglets didn't seem like a big load, and it wasn't like hauling cattle or horses.

She considered herself a rather good driver, but she didn't have much experience with the trailer. She'd been the only one on the ranch that had been able to go, and they wanted to have the pigs there when the first guests arrived on Monday. They had a lot riding on their dude ranch being successful, and she had volunteered to go, just to try to be helpful. Even if it wasn't exactly her area.

Plus, it was a good opportunity for her and Mina to spend some time together and get to know each other. Two hours in the pickup together, and they could chat about anything. Mina wasn't shy. She was outgoing and friendly and chatted up a storm on the way there and the way back.

Obviously, she was a much better pig chaser than Claudia was, so it was a good thing she had her along.

Claudia started out across the street, looking both ways, even though they hadn't seen a single car since they stopped. God had been good that way. She just hoped that they could continue until they had caught all the piglets and no one ran over one or, worse, swerved to miss one and hit something they shouldn't.

"There's one!" Beau said from beside her.

She turned in the direction of his pointed finger and saw he was right.

"There are two," she corrected, hurrying in that direction.

"I'll get ahead of them, cut them off, and if they go back toward you, you can grab them, or I'll sneak up behind them."

She couldn't believe she was actually making plans with Beau. She still wanted him to leave, but she supposed she could use his help catching the piglets first.

"All right," she said as he hurried in front of her to cut the piglets off. They were just moseying down the street, like they were interested in their new surroundings and out for a stroll checking things out. Thankfully they weren't wildly running around, or they would have been long gone by now. Obviously, they were tame piglets.

"Hey, guys. Let's get back on the trailer. Although, I can't blame you for wanting to run away. I bet Miss Claudia has plans to eat you later."

"Would you stop?" she said. "Whose side are you on anyway?" She should have known that he would be on the pigs' side.

A cold nose shoved into her hand, and she looked down to see Ginger looking up at her. Back in her day, Ginger would have been running around, herding the pigs up, and they would have been able to gather all eight of them up without too much trouble at all. Now, while it was obvious that she wanted to help, she hadn't been able to.

"Oh, sweetie. I'm sorry."

"Heads-up!" Beau called, and Claudia glanced up just in time to see the pigs running directly toward her. At least they were running fairly close together, like they didn't want to lose each other.

Ginger crouched, although it was a slow crouch, but still. She moved stiffly from one side to the other as the piglets approached.

Claudia wasn't quite sure how Mina had managed to catch three, because she wasn't sure how to go about grabbing them. Did she jump on top of them? Bend over with her arms out?

Or was there some other technique she hadn't figured out?

She probably spent two seconds trying to figure that out, and by that time, the piglets had gotten to Ginger, who wasn't quite fast enough to turn them around, and they ran directly into Claudia's cowboy boots. She reached down with both hands, sticking her arms around the squirmy little bodies and picking them both up, one in each arm.

Unfortunately, the pigs were facing backward, and she was facing forward, and all she had to leverage them was to hold them tight against her hips.

She was afraid if she walked, they would jiggle loose.

"Mina!" she called.

"I have another one!" Mina called from up the street on the other side of the trailer, where Claudia could not see her.

"I kind of feel like I should be filming this, because I would have a viral video on my hands." Beau came over around the car, humor in his voice as he plucked one of the piglets from under her left arm.

That gave her the leverage to reach over and adjust the other piglet so that she didn't feel like she was going to drop it at any second.

"That would be something you would do, profit off of the suffering of someone else."

"You don't look like you're suffering all that much to me," he said with irony in his voice. "I think the piglets have it much worse."

"You told them I was going to eat them. That was not very nice of you." She had actually found that funny, but she didn't want to admit it.

She grabbed the end of the trailer, opening it wide enough to put the piglet she held inside, closing and then opening it so Beau could get his in.

"Thank you," she said, although the word came out reluctantly. Normally she didn't have a hard time telling people thanks or being grateful, but it was kind of rough being grateful to someone who she felt didn't like her very much at all and who would rather make fun of her and make her life miserable than anything.

"I have one!" Mina said, jogging up to the side of the trailer. Claudia opened the endgate and allowed her to throw it in.

"I think just two more, right?" Mina said. "Did you just put two in?"

"Yeah. If you've gotten four and we've gotten two, then there's just two more."

"All right! I never thought I would be good at chasing piglets, but it's kind of fun," Mina said, her voice chirpy and happy and her posture saying she was having the time of her life.

"She must have her father's personality, since she seems like your opposite. She's so happy," Beau said as Mina skipped away, and Claudia narrowed her eyes. "Where is the dad anyway?" His voice sounded studiously casual.

She wanted to tell him to mind his own business, but this was her opportunity to correct the misconception that he had before.

"She's the daughter of a friend of mine. She's staying with me for the summer. So there. None of my genes are interfering with her happy, sweet disposition."

"You know, if you tried, you'd probably be a really nice person." He sauntered off, and as though mocking her, he called, "Here, piggy, piggy, piggy. Here, piggy, piggy. Come on, bacon, bring your sausages over here."

He was such a dork.

She couldn't help laughing all the same. Except, she stifled it so he wouldn't know. She couldn't let him know that she actually thought he was…funny.

Odd, since she thought of him as rather serious and definitely a jerk. But he'd helped her round up her piglets, and she really couldn't complain about that.

She put a hand on Ginger's faithful head, and they followed him, Ginger and she both walking stiffly, Ginger with her tail up, like she was eager to continue to herd piglets.

And as though his calling had summoned a piglet, it strolled up the opposite sidewalk, like it had taken a little tour of the town and was ready to come back to the trailer.

She paused. Just her luck, he'd probably catch it by himself.

He went around behind the piglet. Maybe he had intended to chase it across the street to her, but Ginger headed it off. It turned around, and the piglet ran right into Beau's arms.

It was disgusting. Except, it was also a relief, because all the piglets were caught. She would have thought they would have been scattered to the four winds by now, and she did appreciate that the Lord had worked it out that they hadn't lost a single one.

"Mina!" she called up the sidewalk where Mina bent over, looking underneath a white pickup parked along the street in front of the diner. "He found it!"

"Nice! And I have the last one. That was fun!" she called, trotting back down the street holding a squealing piglet.

Ginger had come over and stood beside Claudia, and although she was a little put out with her dog for being disloyal, she couldn't be upset with Ginger for long. Ginger had been faithful her entire life.

They met at the back of the trailer as the last pig was loaded and the door closed.

"After all that work, wouldn't it be funny if they all got out again?" Beau said, and Claudia narrowed her eyes at him.

"That would not be funny. Do not even suggest such a thing."

"Are you gonna let me look at your arm?" he asked, although he didn't seem to hold out much hope that she would acquiesce.

She did not. He probably just wanted to scrape it even deeper.

"We'll take care of it when I get home. Thanks for your help." She forced herself to be kind. She could do this.

He jerked his head, gave a little grin to Mina, and said, "I think you might have a career as a pig wrestler. You're pretty good."

"Is there such a thing?" Mina asked, sounding interested.

"I don't know. But if there is, you'll be top notch." With another glance at Claudia, Beau walked back to his truck.

She did not wait to watch him get in but instead said to Mina, "Let's go. The folks at home are gonna wonder where we are."

Grateful that it hadn't taken that long, she went to the front of her truck, helped Ginger in, and started it. It was just her luck that Beau happened along, and as she looked in her side mirror, he blinked his lights at her, indicating she should pull out ahead of him.

She had a good mind to sit there until doomsday, making him go first, but that seemed a little childish. So, she put her turn signal on and pulled out.

"Oh!" Mina said almost immediately. "We missed one!"

But no, as she hit the brakes, the trailer door slammed against the trailer, and she realized that Beau must have unlatched it while he was standing there with his hand on it. Or maybe never latched it to begin with.

And as she watched in the mirror, all eight piglets filed out from behind the trailer and ran down the street of Sweet Water again.

She was going to be hard-pressed not to murder someone.

Sign up for Jessie's newsletter! Get a free book, access to exclusive bonus content, get fun and funny updates on her life on the farm and more!

A Gift from Jessie

View this code through your smart phone camera to be taken to a page where you can download a FREE ebook when you sign up to get updates from Jessie Gussman! Find out why people say, "Jessie's is the only newsletter I open and read" and "You make my day brighter. Love, love, love reading your newsletters. I don't know where you find time to write books. You are so busy living life. A true blessing." and "I know from now on that I can't be drinking my morning coffee while reading your newsletter – I laughed so hard I sprayed it out all over the table!"

Claim your free book from Jessie!

Escape to more faith-filled romance series by Jessie Gussman!

The Complete Sweet Water, North Dakota Reading Order:

Series One: Sweet Water Ranch Western Cowboy Romance (11 book series)

Series Two: Coming Home to North Dakota (12 book series)

Series Three: Flyboys of Sweet Briar Ranch in North Dakota (13 book series)

Series Four: Sweet View Ranch Western Cowboy Romance (10 book series)

Spinoffs and More! Additional Series You'll Love:

Jessie's First Series: Sweet Haven Farm (4 book series)

Small-Town Romance: The Baxter Boys (5 book series)

Bad-Boy Sweet Romance: Richmond Rebels Sweet Romance (3 book series)

Sweet Water Spinoff: Cowboy Crossing (9 book series)

Small Town Romantic Comedy: Good Grief, Idaho (5 book series)

True Stories from Jessie's Farm: Stories from Jessie Gussman's Newsletter (3 book series)

Reader-Favorite! Sweet Beach Romance: Blueberry Beach (8 book series)

Blueberry Beach Spinoff: Strawberry Sands (10 book series)

From Strawberry Sands to: Raspberry Ridge (12 book series)
Swoonfully Jolly Holiday Stories:
Holiday Romance: Cowboy Mountain Christmas (6 book series)
Cowboy Mountain Christmas Spinoff: A Heartland Cowboy Christmas (9 book series)
New and Much Loved: Mistletoe Meadows (4 books and counting!)
Laughing Through the Snow: Christmas Tree, PA Sweet Romcoms (6 short reads)